A NEWBERY CHRISTMAS

A NEWBERY CHRISTMAS

Fourteen
stories of Christmas
by Newbery Award–winning
authors

Selected by
Martin H. Greenberg
and
Charles G. Waugh

Introduction by Carol-Lynn Rössel Waugh

DELACORTE PRESS/NEW YORK

Published by Delacorte Press
Bantam Doubleday Dell Publishing Group, Inc.
666 Fifth Avenue   New York, New York 10103

Acknowledgments

"Babouscka," a Russian legend from FAVORITE STORIES FOR THE CHILDREN'S HOUR, edited by Carolyn Sherwin Bailey and Clara M. Lewis, copyright © 1965 by Platt & Munk. Reprinted by permission of Grosset & Dunlap.

"The Hundred Dresses" by Eleanor Estes. From THE HUNDRED DRESSES, copyright 1944 by Harcourt Brace Jovanovich, Inc., and renewed 1971 by Eleanor Estes and Louis Slobodkin. Reprinted by permission of the author.

"A Letter from Santa Claus" by Eleanor Estes. From THE MIDDLE MOFFAT, copyright 1942 and renewed 1970 by Eleanor Estes. Reprinted by permission of Harcourt Brace Jovanovich, Inc.

"Eliot Miles Does Not Wish You a Merry Christmas Because . . ." by E. L. Konigsburg. Copyright © 1971 by E. L. Konigsburg. Reprinted by permission of the author.

"A Full House" by Madeleine L'Engle. Copyright © 1980 by Madeleine L'Engle. Reprinted by permission of Lescher & Lescher, Ltd.

"Once in the Year" by Elizabeth Yates. Copyright © 1991 by Upper Room Books. Reprinted by permission of the author.

"The Merry History of a Christmas Pie" by Nancy Willard. Copyright © 1991 by Nancy Willard. Reprinted by permission of the author.

"The Christmas Fake" by Lois Lenski. Copyright © 1968 by Lois Lenski. Reprinted by permission of Moses & Singer on behalf of the Lois Lenski Covey Foundation.

"Woodrow Kennington Works Practically a Miracle" by Katherine Paterson. Copyright © 1979 by Thomas Y. Crowell. Reprinted by permission of the publisher.

"All Through the Night" by Rachel Field. Copyright 1940 by Rachel Field. Reprinted by permission of Radcliffe College.

"The Christmas Apple" by Ruth Sawyer. Copyright 1916 by Ruth Sawyer. Reprinted by permission of the Estate of Ruth Sawyer.

"A Candle for St. Bridget" by Ruth Sawyer. Copyright 1923 by Ruth Sawyer. Reprinted by permission of the Estate of Ruth Sawyer.

"The Galloping Sleigh" by Hugh Lofting. Copyright 1927 by Hugh Lofting. Reprinted by permission of Christopher Lofting.

"Ramona, the Sheep Suit, and the Three Wise Persons" by Beverly Cleary. Copyright © 1975 by Beverly Cleary. Reprinted by permission of William Morrow and Company, Inc.

Library of Congress Cataloging in Publication Data

A Newbery Christmas : fourteen stories of Christmas by Newbery Award–winning authors / selected by Martin H. Greenberg and Charles G. Waugh : introduction by Carol-Lynn Rössel Waugh.
    p.   cm.
    Summary: A collection of stories about Christmas, by Newbery Award–winning authors such as Eleanor Estes, E. L. Konigsburg, Madeleine L'Engle, and Katherine Paterson.
    ISBN 0-385-30485-4
    1. Christmas—Juvenile fiction.   2. Children's stories, America. [1. Christmas—Fiction. 2. Short stories.] I. Greenberg, Martin. II. Waugh, Charles.
PZ5.N39 1991
813'.010833—dc20
[Fic]   91-17124 CIP AC

Manufactured in the United States of America
November 1991
10 9 8 7 6 5 4 3

TABLE OF CONTENTS

Contents

Carol-Lynn Rössel Waugh

INTRODUCTION

"Come with me in Merry Measure
While I tell of Yuletide Treasure. . . .
Come with me in Mary's Manger
While I tell of Yuletide Danger."

EVERY YEAR come Christmastime, as I sang in the junior choir at St. Stephen's Church, the alternate verses to "Deck the Halls" intrigued me. Hymn books showed one or the other, never both. What kind of yuletide treasure, what kind of yuletide danger were they promising? I wanted both, and got none; the songwriter never made good on his promise.

My mind filled the gaps, melding half-remembered stories with secret wishes, and I knew I'd find that Christmas treasure, that Christmas magic, if only I looked hard enough. I was of two minds, however, about the promised Christmas danger.

The short, brisk days and long, cold midwinter nights of Christmastide are a time when imaginations, young and old, are prone to twisting a flickering shadow, a sudden blast of wind, or a silvery pathway cast by a full moon into creatures of wonder and awe. At such a time, who can say for certain that animals cannot speak, that reindeer cannot fly?

I knew they did; and that knowledge was so deep-seated that I can close my eyes, even now, and feel my five- or six-year-old self creeping out of bed to stand at my bedroom window in the house my great-grandfather built on the Staten Island shore. Outside, sparkling over the waters of the Arthur Kill, the lights of the Outerbridge Crossing linking the Island to New Jersey twinkled like a diamond and ruby chain. I was certain if I waited long enough, I'd see Santa and his sleigh swoop over them, riding the strand of lights like a roller-coaster car.

I never waited long enough. But I still believed. Even when I was in high school, when it was fashionable to put away childish ideas, I peeked at the Christmas bridge—just in case. I believed in its magic, and for me, like Tinker Bell, it lived then, and—I'll admit it—it still does.

Unlike most of my peers, who forsook childish things in adulthood, I made a career of them. While they do Serious Business, I design and photograph teddy bears and dolls. Most of all, I write: stories for children and books and articles about toys (and other things) for adults who now regret having spurned their Christmas toys.

When I grew old enough to have children, I told them about my Christmas window, continuing the tradition begun with the most magical Christmas story of all: that of the child Jesus, his birth, and his amazing birthday party.

Wherever Christianity has taken hold, the Christmas legend, through almost two thousand years has been embraced, adopted, and adapted by the land and people who tell it.

Italians tell of Befana, the gift-bearing Tuscan Christmas witch; Russians tell of Babouscka, the old woman who never stops searching for the baby prince, distributing the gifts meant for him to mortal children.

On this most child-centered holiday, the best of these stories are told for children, the very best of them acting as time capsules, transporting listeners back, rekindling tastes and smells, memories and emotions. At Christmas, nostalgia reigns; children demand, "Tell us how it was in the good old days." And, whether those days were a decade or a century ago, we comply.

Continuing in this tradition, Marty and my husband, Charles, have chosen fourteen such tales written by twelve master American storytellers—one for each of the days of Christmas. These writers are especially skilled at spinning tales for children, for they are all winners of the John Newbery Medal, the highest achievement in American children's literature; only one is awarded in any given year.

These Christmas tales range from traditional to contemporary, from hilarious to heart-tugging, and we guarantee at least some of them will resonate with your own half-forgotten memories.

Great writers write on several levels, so this book is for everyone. If you're an adult, enjoy reading the stories for the nostalgia, for the time-capsule voyage they offer into your youth; you'll find they're written with the adult in mind.

If you're a teenager, you can read them for yourself: they were, most of all, written with you in mind.

And if you have young ones, just beginning to discover the wonders of Christmas treasures and Christmas dangers, don't just read them, share them. Then tell anew a Christmas tale from your own olden days, to pass the memory on.

And if you do, you may find your children, as I found mine one Christmas Eve, standing by a familiar bedroom window, checking out your diamond-and-ruby-chained bridge to see if reindeer just might fly.

A NEWBERY CHRISTMAS

Carolyn Sherwin Bailey

BABOUSCKA

IT WAS the night the dear Christ Child came to Bethlehem. In a country far away from Him, an old woman named Babouscka sat in her snug little house by her warm fire. The wind was drifting the snow outside and howling down the chimney, but it only made Babouscka's fire burn more brightly.

"How glad I am that I may stay indoors!" said Babouscka, holding her hands out to the bright blaze.

But suddenly she heard a loud rap at her door. She opened it and her candle shone on three old men standing outside in the snow. Their beards were as white as the snow, and so long that they reached the ground. Their eyes shone kindly in the light of Babouscka's candle, and their arms were full of precious things—boxes of jewels, and sweet-smelling oils, and ointments.

"We have traveled far, Babouscka," they said, "and we stop to tell you of the Baby Prince born this night in Bethlehem. He comes to rule the world and teach all men to be loving and true. We carry Him gifts. Come with us, Babouscka!"

But Babouscka looked at the driving snow, and then inside at her cozy room and the crackling fire.

"It is too late to go with you, good sirs," she said. "The weather is too cold."

She went inside again and shut the door, and the old men journeyed on to Bethlehem without her. But as Babouscka sat by her fire, rocking, she began to think about the little Christ Child, for she loved all babies.

"Tomorrow I will go to find Him," she said—"tomorrow, when it is light. And I will carry Him some toys."

So when it was morning Babouscka put on her long cloak, and took her staff, and filled her basket with the pretty things a baby would like—gold balls, and wooden toys, and strings of silver cobwebs—and she set out to find the Christ Child.

But, oh! Babouscka had forgotten to ask the three old men the road to Bethlehem, and they had traveled so far through the night that she could not overtake them. Up and down the roads she hurried, through woods and fields and towns, saying to whomsoever she met:

"I go to find the Christ Child. Where does He lie? I bring some pretty toys for His sake."

But no one could tell her the way to go, and they all said, "Farther on, Babouscka, farther on."

So she traveled on, and on, and on for years and years —but she never found the little Christ Child.

They say that old Babouscka is traveling still, looking for Him. When it comes Christmas Eve, and the children are lying fast asleep, Babouscka comes softly through the snowy fields and towns, wrapped in her long cloak and carrying her basket on her arm. With her staff she raps gently at the doors and goes inside and holds her candle close to the children's faces.

"Is He here?" she asks. "Is the little Christ Child here?" And then she turns sorrowfully away again, crying, "Farther on, farther on." But before she leaves, she takes a toy from her basket and lays it beside the pillow for a Christmas gift. "For His sake," she says softly, and then hurries on through the years and forever in search of the little Christ Child.

Eleanor Estes

THE HUNDRED DRESSES

ODAY, MONDAY, Wanda Petronski was not
in her seat. But nobody, not even Peggy and Made-
line, the girls who started all the fun, noticed her
absence.

Usually Wanda sat in the next to the last seat in the
last row in Room 13. She sat in the corner of the room
where the rough boys who did not make good marks on
their report cards sat; the corner of the room where there
was most scuffling of feet, most roars of laughter when anything funny was said, and most mud and dirt on the floor.

Wanda did not sit there because she was rough and
noisy. On the contrary she was very quiet and rarely said
anything at all. And nobody had ever heard her laugh out

loud. Sometimes she twisted her mouth into a crooked sort of smile, but that was all.

Nobody knew exactly why Wanda sat in that seat unless it was because she came all the way from Boggins Heights, and her feet were usually caked with dry mud that she picked up coming down the country roads. Maybe the teacher liked to keep all the children who were apt to come in with dirty shoes in one corner of the room. But no one really thought much about Wanda Petronski once she was in the classroom. The time they thought about her was outside of school hours, at noontime when they were coming back to school, or in the morning early before school began, when groups of two or three or even more would be talking and laughing on their way to the school yard.

Then sometimes they waited for Wanda—to have fun with her.

The next day, Tuesday, Wanda was not in school either. And nobody noticed her absence again, except the teacher and probably big Bill Byron, who sat in the seat behind Wanda's and who could now put his long legs around her empty desk, one on each side, and sit there like a frog, to the great entertainment of all in his corner of the room.

But on Wednesday, Peggy and Maddie, who sat in the front row along with other children who got good marks and didn't track in a whole lot of mud, did notice that Wanda wasn't there. Peggy was the most popular girl in school. She was pretty; she had many pretty clothes and her auburn hair was curly. Maddie was her closest friend.

The reason Peggy and Maddie noticed Wanda's absence was because Wanda had made them late to school. They had waited and waited for Wanda—to have some fun with her—and she just hadn't come. They kept thinking she'd come any minute. They saw Jack Beggles running to school, his necktie askew and his cap at a precarious tilt. They knew it must be late, for he always managed to slide into his chair exactly when the bell rang as though he were making a touchdown. Still they waited one minute more and one minute more, hoping she'd come. But finally they had to race off without seeing her.

The two girls reached their classroom after the doors had been closed. The children were reciting in unison the Gettysburg Address, for that was the way Miss Mason always began the session. Peggy and Maddie slipped into their seats just as the class was saying the last lines . . . "that these dead shall not have died in vain; that the nation shall, under God, have a new birth of freedom, and that government of the people, by the people, for the people, shall not perish from the earth."

After Peggy and Maddie stopped feeling like intruders in a class that had already begun, they looked across the room and noticed that Wanda was not in her seat. Furthermore her desk was dusty and looked as though she hadn't been there yesterday either. Come to think of it, they hadn't seen her yesterday. They had waited for her a little while but had forgotten about her when they reached school.

They often waited for Wanda Petronski—to have fun with her.

Wanda lived way up on Boggins Heights, and Boggins

Heights was no place to live. It was a good place to go and pick wild flowers in the summer, but you always held your breath till you got safely past old man Svenson's yellow house. People in the town said old man Svenson was no good. He didn't work and, worse still, his house and yard were disgracefully dirty, with rusty tin cans strewn about and even an old straw hat. He lived alone with his dog and his cat. No wonder, said the people of the town. Who would live with him? And many stories circulated about him and the stories were the kind that made people scurry past his house even in broad daylight and hope not to meet him.

Beyond Svenson's there were a few small scattered frame houses, and in one of these Wanda Petronski lived with her father and her brother Jake.

Wanda Petronski. Most of the children in Room 13 didn't have names like that. They had names easy to say, like Thomas, Smith, or Allen. There was one boy named Bounce, Willie Bounce, and people thought that was funny but not funny in the same way that Petronski was.

Wanda didn't have any friends. She came to school alone and went home alone. She always wore a faded blue dress that didn't hang right. It was clean, but it looked as though it had never been ironed properly. She didn't have any friends, but a lot of girls talked to her. They waited for her under the maple trees on the corner of Oliver Street. Or they surrounded her in the school yard as she stood watching some little girls play hopscotch on the worn hard ground.

"Wanda," Peggy would say in a most courteous manner, as though she were talking to Miss Mason or to the principal perhaps. "Wanda," she'd say, giving one of her friends a nudge, "tell us. How many dresses did you say you had hanging up in your closet?"

"A hundred," said Wanda.

"A hundred!" exclaimed all the girls incredulously, and the little girls would stop playing hopscotch and listen.

"Yeah, a hundred, all lined up," said Wanda. Then her thin lips drew together in silence.

"What are they like? All silk, I bet," said Peggy.

"Yeah, all silk, all colors."

"Velvet too?"

"Yeah, velvet too. A hundred dresses," repeated Wanda stolidly. "All lined up in my closet."

Then they'd let her go. And then before she'd gone very far, they couldn't help bursting into shrieks and peals of laughter.

A hundred dresses! Obviously the only dress Wanda had was the blue one she wore every day. So what did she say she had a hundred for? What a story! And the girls laughed derisively, while Wanda moved over to the sunny place by the ivy-covered brick wall of the school building where she usually stood and waited for the bell to ring.

But if the girls had met her at the corner of Oliver Street, they'd carry her along with them for a way, stopping every few feet for more incredulous questions. And it wasn't always dresses they talked about. Sometimes it was hats, or coats, or even shoes.

"How many shoes did you say you had?"

"Sixty."

"Sixty! Sixty pairs or sixty shoes?"

"Sixty pairs. All lined up in my closet."

"Yesterday you said fifty."

"Now I got sixty."

Cries of exaggerated politeness greeted this.

"All alike?" said the girls.

"Oh, no. Every pair is different. All colors. All lined up." And Wanda would shift her eyes quickly from Peggy to a distant spot, as though she were looking far ahead, looking but not seeing anything.

Then the outer fringe of the crowd of girls would break away gradually, laughing, and little by little, in pairs, the group would disperse. Peggy, who had thought up this game, and Maddie, her inseparable friend, were always the last to leave. And finally Wanda would move up the street, her eyes dull and her mouth closed tight, hitching her left shoulder every now and then in the funny way she had, finishing the walk to school alone.

Peggy was not really cruel. She protected small children from bullies. And she cried for hours if she saw an animal mistreated. If anybody had said to her, "Don't you think that is a cruel way to treat Wanda?" she would have been very surprised. Cruel? What did the girl want to go and say she had a hundred dresses for? Anybody could tell that was a lie. Why did she want to lie? And she wasn't just an ordinary person, else why would she have a name like that? Anyway, they never made her cry.

As for Maddie, this business of asking Wanda every day how many dresses and how many hats and how many this and that she had was bothering her. Maddie was poor herself. She usually wore somebody's hand-me-down clothes. Thank goodness, she didn't live up on Boggins Heights or have a funny name. And her forehead didn't shine the way Wanda's round one did. What did she use on it? Sapolio? That's what all the girls wanted to know.

Sometimes when Peggy was asking Wanda those questions in that mock polite voice, Maddie felt embarrassed and studied the marbles in the palm of her hand, rolling them around and saying nothing herself. Not that she felt sorry for Wanda exactly. She would never have paid any attention to Wanda if Peggy hadn't invented the dresses game. But suppose Peggy and all the others started in on her next! She wasn't as poor as Wanda perhaps, but she was poor. Of course she would have more sense than to say a hundred dresses. Still she would not like them to begin on her. Not at all! Oh, dear! She did wish Peggy would stop teasing Wanda Petronski.

Somehow Maddie could not buckle down to work.

She sharpened her pencil, turning it around carefully in the little red sharpener, letting the shavings fall in a neat heap on a piece of scrap paper, and trying not to get any of the dust from the lead on her clean arithmetic paper.

A slight frown puckered her forehead. In the first place she didn't like being late to school. And in the second place she kept thinking about Wanda. Somehow Wanda's desk, though empty, seemed to be the only thing she saw when she looked over to that side of the room.

How had the hundred dresses game begun in the first place, she asked herself impatiently. It was hard to remember the time when they hadn't played that game with

Wanda; hard to think all the way back from now, when the hundred dresses was like the daily dozen, to then, when everything seemed much nicer. Oh, yes. She remembered. It had begun that day when Cecile first wore her new red dress. Suddenly the whole scene flashed swiftly and vividly before Maddie's eyes.

It was a bright blue day in September. No, it must have been October, because when she and Peggy were coming to school, arms around each other and singing, Peggy had said, "You know what? This must be the kind of day they mean when they say, 'October's bright blue weather.'"

Maddie remembered that because afterwards it didn't seem like bright blue weather any more, although the weather had not changed in the slightest.

As they turned from shady Oliver Street into Maple, they both blinked. For now the morning sun shone straight in their eyes. Besides that, bright flashes of color came from a group of a half-dozen or more girls across the street. Their sweaters and jackets and dresses, blues and golds and reds, and one crimson one in particular, caught the sun's rays like bright pieces of glass.

A crisp, fresh wind was blowing, swishing their skirts and blowing their hair in their eyes. The girls were all exclaiming and shouting and each one was trying to talk louder than the others. Maddie and Peggy joined the group, and the laughing, and the talking.

"Hi, Peg! Hi, Maddie!" they were greeted warmly. "Look at Cecile!"

What they were all exclaiming about was the dress that

Cecile had on—a crimson dress with cap and socks to match. It was a bright new dress and very pretty. Everyone was admiring it and admiring Cecile. For long, slender Cecile was a toe-dancer and wore fancier clothes than most of them. And she had her black satin bag with her precious white satin ballet slippers slung over her shoulders. Today was the day for her dancing lesson.

Maddie sat down on the granite curbstone to tie her shoelaces. She listened happily to what they were saying. They all seemed especially jolly today, probably because it was such a bright day. Everything sparkled. Way down at the end of the street the sun shimmered and turned to silver the blue water of the bay. Maddie picked up a piece of broken mirror and flashed a small circle of light edged with rainbow colors onto the houses, the trees, and the top of the telegraph pole.

And it was then that Wanda had come along with her brother Jake.

They didn't often come to school together. Jake had to get to school very early because he helped old Mr. Heany, the school janitor, with the furnace, or raking up the dry leaves, or other odd jobs before school opened. Today he must be late.

Even Wanda looked pretty in this sunshine, and her pale blue dress looked like a piece of the sky in summer; and that old gray toboggan cap she wore—it must be something Jake had found—looked almost jaunty. Maddie watched them absent-mindedly as she flashed her piece of broken mirror here and there. And only absent-mindedly she noticed Wanda stop short when they reached the crowd of laughing and shouting girls.

"Come on," Maddie heard Jake say. "I gotta hurry. I gotta get the doors open and ring the bell."

"You go the rest of the way," said Wanda. "I want to stay here."

Jake shrugged and went on up Maple Street. Wanda slowly approached the group of girls. With each step forward, before she put her foot down she seemed to hesitate for a long, long time. She approached the group as a timid animal might, ready to run if anything alarmed it.

Even so, Wanda's mouth was twisted into the vaguest suggestion of a smile. She must feel happy too because everybody must feel happy on such a day.

As Wanda joined the outside fringe of girls, Maddie stood up too and went over close to Peggy to get a good look at Cecile's new dress herself. She forgot about Wanda, and more girls kept coming up, enlarging the group and all exclaiming about Cecile's new dress.

"Isn't it lovely!" said one.

"Yeah, I have a new blue dress, but it's not as pretty as that," said another.

"My mother just bought me a plaid, one of the Stuart plaids."

"I got a new dress for dancing school."

"I'm gonna make my mother get me one just like Cecile's."

Everyone was talking to everyone else. Nobody said anything to Wanda, but there she was, a part of the crowd. The girls closed in a tighter circle around Cecile, still talk-

had some fun with Wanda, winning the approving laughter of the girls.

Yes, that was the way it had all begun, the game of the hundred dresses. It all happened so suddenly and unexpectedly, with everybody falling right in, that even if you felt uncomfortable as Maddie had there wasn't anything you could do about it. Maddie wagged her head up and down. Yes, she repeated to herself, that was the way it began, that day, that bright blue day.

And she wrapped up her shavings and went to the front of the room to empty them in the teacher's basket.

Now today, even though she and Peggy had been late to school, Maddie was glad she had not had to make fun of Wanda. She worked her arithmetic problems absent-mindedly. Eight times eight . . . let's see . . . nothing she could do about making fun of Wanda. She wished she had the nerve to write Peggy a note, because she knew she'd never have the courage to speak right out to Peggy, to say, "Hey, Peg, let's stop asking Wanda how many dresses she has."

When she finished her arithmetic, she did start a note to Peggy. Suddenly she paused and shuddered. She pictured herself in the school yard, a new target for Peggy and the girls. Peggy might ask her where she got the dress she had on, and Maddie would have to say that it was one of Peggy's old ones that Maddie's mother had tried to disguise with new trimmings so that no one in Room 13 would recognize it.

If only Peggy would decide of her own accord to stop

having fun with Wanda. Oh, well! Maddie ran her hand through her short blond hair as though to push the uncomfortable thoughts away. What difference did it make? Slowly Maddie tore the note she had started into bits. She was Peggy's best friend, and Peggy was the best-liked girl in the whole room. Peggy could not possibly do anything that was really wrong, she thought.

As for Wanda, she was just some girl who lived up on Boggins Heights and stood alone in the school yard. Nobody in the room thought about Wanda at all except when it was her turn to stand up for oral reading. Then they all hoped she would hurry up and finish and sit down, because it took her forever to read a paragraph. Sometimes she stood up and just looked at her book and couldn't, or wouldn't, read at all. The teacher tried to help her, but she'd just stand there until the teacher told her to sit down. Was she dumb or what? Maybe she was just timid. The only time she talked was in the school yard about her hundred dresses. Maddie remembered her telling about one of her dresses, a pale blue one with cerise-colored trimmings. And she remembered another that was brilliant jungle green with a red sash. "You'd look like a Christmas tree in that," the girls had said in pretended admiration.

Thinking about Wanda and her hundred dresses all lined up in the closet, Maddie began to wonder who was going to win the drawing and color contest. For girls, this contest consisted of designing dresses, and for boys, of designing motor boats. Probably Peggy would win the girls' medal. Peggy drew better than anyone else in the room. At least that's what everybody thought. You should see the way she could copy a picture in a magazine or some film star's head. You could almost tell who it was. Oh, Maddie did hope Peggy would win. Hope so? She was sure Peggy would win. Well, tomorrow the teacher was going to announce the winners. Then they'd know.

Thoughts of Wanda sank further and further from Maddie's mind, and by the time the history lesson began she had forgotten all about her.

The next day it was drizzling. Maddie and Peggy hurried to school under Peggy's umbrella. Naturally on a day like this they didn't wait for Wanda Petronski on the corner of Oliver Street, the street that far, far away, under the railroad tracks and up the hill, led to Boggins Heights. Anyway they weren't taking chances on being late today, because today was important.

"Do you think Miss Mason will surely announce the winners today?" asked Peggy.

"Oh, I hope so, the minute we get in," said Maddie, and added, "Of course you'll win, Peg."

"Hope so," said Peggy eagerly.

The minute they entered the classroom they stopped short and gasped. There were drawings all over the room, on every ledge and window sill, tacked to the tops of the blackboards, spread over the bird charts, dazzling colors and brilliant lavish designs, all drawn on great sheets of wrapping paper.

There must have been a hundred of them all lined up!

These must be the drawings for the contest. They

were! Everybody stopped and whistled or murmured admiringly.

As soon as the class had assembled Miss Mason announced the winners. Jack Beggles had won for the boys, she said, and his design of an outboard motor boat was on exhibition in Room 12, along with the sketches by all the other boys.

"As for the girls," she said, "although just one or two sketches were submitted by most, one girl—and Room 13 should be very proud of her—this one girl actually drew one hundred designs—all different and all beautiful. In the opinion of the judges, any one of her drawings is worthy of winning the prize. I am happy to say that Wanda Petronski is the winner of the girls' medal. Unfortunately Wanda has been absent from school for some days and is not here to receive the applause that is due her. Let us hope she will be back tomorrow. Now, class, you may file around the room quietly and look at her exquisite drawings."

The children burst into applause, and even the boys were glad to have a chance to stamp on the floor, put their fingers in their mouths and whistle, though they were not interested in the dresses. Maddie and Peggy were among the first to reach the blackboard to look at the drawings.

"Look, Peg," whispered Maddie, "there's that blue one she told us about. Isn't it beautiful?"

"Yeah," said Peggy, "and here's that green one. Boy, and I thought I could draw!"

While the class was circling the room, the monitor from the principal's office brought Miss Mason a note. Miss Mason read it several times and studied it thoughtfully for a while. Then she clapped her hands and said, "Attention, class. Everyone back to his seat."

When the shuffling of feet had stopped and the room was still and quiet, Miss Mason said, "I have a letter from Wanda's father that I want to read to you."

Miss Mason stood there a moment and the silence in the room grew tense and expectant. The teacher adjusted her glasses slowly and deliberately. Her manner indicated that what was coming—this letter from Wanda's father— was a matter of great importance. Everybody listened closely as Miss Mason read the brief note:

"Dear teacher: My Wanda will not come to your school any more. Jake also. Now we move away to big city. No more holler Polack. No more ask why funny name. Plenty of funny names in the big city. Yours truly,
Jan Petronski."

A deep silence met the reading of this letter. Miss Mason took her glasses off, blew on them and wiped them on her soft white handkerchief. Then she put them on again and looked at the class. When she spoke her voice was very low.

"I am sure none of my boys and girls in Room 13 would purposely and deliberately hurt anyone's feelings because his name happened to be a long unfamiliar one. I prefer to think that what was said was said in thoughtlessness. I know that all of you feel the way I do, that this is a very unfortunate thing to have happen. Unfortunate and sad, both. And I want you all to think about it."

The first period was a study period. Maddie tried to prepare her lessons, but she could not put her mind on her work. She had a very sick feeling in the bottom of her stomach. True, she had not enjoyed listening to Peggy ask Wanda how many dresses she had in her closet, but she had said nothing. She had stood by silently, and that was just as bad as what Peggy had done. Worse. She was a coward. At least Peggy hadn't considered they were being mean, but she, Maddie, had thought they were doing wrong. She had thought, supposing she was the one being made fun of. She could put herself in Wanda's shoes. But she had done just as much as Peggy to make life miserable for Wanda by simply standing by and saying nothing. She had helped to make someone so unhappy that she had had to move away from town.

Goodness! Wasn't there anything she could do? If only she could tell Wanda she hadn't meant to hurt her feelings. She turned around and stole a glance at Peggy, but Peggy did not look up. She seemed to be studying hard.

Well, whether Peggy felt badly or not, she, Maddie, had to do something. She had to find Wanda Petronski. Maybe she had not yet moved away. Maybe Peggy would climb the Heights with her and they would tell Wanda she had won the contest. And that they thought she was smart and the hundred dresses were beautiful.

When school was dismissed in the afternoon, Peggy said with pretended casualness, "Hey, let's go and see if that kid has left town or not."

So Peggy had had the same idea as Maddie had had!

Maddie glowed. Peggy was really all right, just as she always thought. Peg was really all right. She was o.k.

The two girls hurried out of the building, up the street toward Boggins Heights, the part of town that wore such a forbidding air on this kind of a November afternoon, drizzly, damp, and dismal.

"Well, at least," said Peggy gruffly, "I never did call her a foreigner or make fun of her name. I never thought she had the sense to know we were making fun of her anyway. I thought she was too dumb. And gee, look how she can draw! And I thought I could draw."

Maddie could say nothing. All she hoped was that they would find Wanda. Just so she'd be able to tell her they were sorry they had all picked on her. And just to say how wonderful the whole school thought she was, and please not to move away and everybody would be nice. She and Peggy would fight anybody who was not nice.

Maddie fell to imagining a story in which she and Peggy assailed any bully who might be going to pick on Wanda. "Petronski—Onski!" somebody would yell, and she and Peggy would pounce on the guilty one. For a time Maddie consoled herself with these thoughts, but they soon vanished and again she felt unhappy and wished everything could be nice the way it was before any of them had made fun of Wanda.

Br-r-r! How drab and cold and cheerless it was up here on the Heights! In the summer time the woods, the sumac, and the ferns that grew along the brook on the side of the road were lush and made this a beautiful walk on Sunday afternoons. But now it did not seem beautiful. The brook

had shrunk to the merest trickle, and today's drizzle sharpened the outlines of the rusty tin cans, old shoes, and for-
lorn remnants of a big black umbrella in the bed of the
brook.

The two girls hurried on. They hoped to get to the top
of the hill before dark. Otherwise they were not certain
they could find Wanda's house. At last, puffing and pant-
ing, they rounded the top of the hill. The first house, that
old rickety one, belonged to old man Svenson. Peggy and
Maddie hurried past it almost on tiptoe. Somebody said
once that old man Svenson had shot a man. Others said
"Nonsense! He's an old good-for-nothing. Wouldn't hurt a
flea."

But, false or true, the girls breathed more freely as they
rounded the corner. It was too cold and drizzly for old man
Svenson to be in his customary chair tilted against the
house, chewing and spitting tobacco juice. Even his dog was
nowhere in sight and had not barked at the girls from
wherever he might be.

"I think that's where the Petronskis live," said Maddie, pointing to a little white house with lots of chicken
coops at the side of it. Wisps of old grass stuck up here and
there along the pathway like thin wet kittens. The house
and its sparse little yard looked shabby but clean. It re-
minded Maddie of Wanda's one dress, her faded blue cotton dress, shabby but clean.

There was not a sign of life about the house except for
a yellow cat, half grown, crouching on the one small step
close to the front door. It leapt timidly with a small cry half
way up a tree when the girls came into the yard. Peggy

knocked firmly on the door, but there was no answer. She and Maddie went around to the back yard and knocked there. Still there was no answer.

"Wanda!" called Peggy. They listened sharply, but only a deep silence pressed against their eardrums. There was no doubt about it. The Petronskis were gone. "Maybe they just went away for a little while and haven't really left with their furniture yet," suggested Maddie hopefully. Maddie was beginning to wonder how she could bear the hard fact that Wanda had actually gone and that she might never be able to make amends.

"Well," said Peggy, "let's see if the door is open."

They cautiously turned the knob of the front door. It opened easily, for it was a light thing and looked as though it furnished but frail protection against the cold winds that blew up here in the winter time. The little square room that the door opened into was empty. There was absolutely nothing left in it, and in the corner a closet with its door wide open was empty too. Maddie wondered what it had held before the Petronskis moved out. And she thought of Wanda saying, "Sure, a hundred dresses . . . all lined up in the closet."

Well, anyway, real and imaginary dresses alike were gone. The Petronskis were gone. And now how could she and Peggy tell Wanda anything? Maybe the teacher knew where she had moved to. Maybe old man Svenson knew. They might knock on his door and ask on the way down. Or the post office might know. If they wrote a letter, Wanda might get it because the post office might forward it. Feeling very downcast and discouraged, the girls closed the door and started for home. Coming down the road, way off in the distance, through the drizzle they could see the water of the bay, gray and cold.

"Do you suppose that was their cat and they forgot her?" asked Peggy. But the cat wasn't anywhere around now, and as the girls turned the bend they saw her crouching under the dilapidated wooden chair in front of old man Svenson's house. So perhaps the cat belonged to him. They lost their courage about knocking on his door and asking when the Petronskis had left and anyway, goodness! here was old man Svenson himself coming up the road. Everything about Svenson was yellow; his house, his cat, his trousers, his drooping mustache and tangled hair, his hound loping behind him, and the long streams of tobacco juice he expertly shot from between his scattered yellow teeth. The two girls drew over to the side of the path as they hurried by. When they were a good way past, they stopped.

"Hey, Mr. Svenson!" yelled Peggy. "When did the Petronskis move?"

Old man Svenson turned around, but said nothing. Finally he did answer, but his words were unintelligible, and the two girls turned and ran down the hill as fast as they could. Old man Svenson looked after them for a moment and then went on up the hill, muttering to himself and scratching his head.

When they were back down on Oliver Street again, the girls stopped running. They still felt disconsolate, and Maddie wondered if she was going to be unhappy about Wanda and the hundred dresses forever. Nothing would ever seem good to her again, because just when she was about to enjoy something—like going for a hike with Peggy to look for bayberries or sliding down Barley Hill—she'd bump right smack into the thought that she had made Wanda Petronski move away.

"Well, anyway," said Peggy, "she's gone now, so what can we do? Besides, when I was asking her about all of her dresses she probably was getting good ideas for her drawings. She might not even have won the contest otherwise."

Maddie carefully turned this idea over in her head, for if there was anything in it she would not have to feel so bad. But that night she could not get to sleep. She thought about Wanda and her faded blue dress and the little house she had lived in; and old man Svenson living a few steps away. And she thought of the glowing picture those hundred dresses made—all lined up in the classroom.

At last Maddie sat up in bed and pressed her forehead tight in her hands and really thought. This was the hardest thinking she had ever done. After a long, long time she reached an important conclusion.

She was never going to stand by and say nothing again.

If she ever heard anybody picking on someone because they were funny looking or because they had strange names, she'd speak up. Even if it meant losing Peggy's friendship. She had no way of making things right with Wanda, but from now on she would never make anybody else so unhappy again. Finally, all tired out, Maddie fell asleep.

. . .

On Saturday Maddie spent the afternoon with Peggy. They were writing a letter to Wanda Petronski.

It was just a friendly letter telling about the contest and telling Wanda she had won. They told her how pretty her drawings were, and that now they were studying about Winfield Scott in school. And they asked her if she liked where she was living now and if she liked her new teacher. They had meant to say they were sorry, but it ended up with their just writing a friendly letter, the kind they would have written to any good friend, and they signed it with lots of X's for love.

They mailed the letter to Boggins Heights, writing "Please Forward" on the envelope. The teacher had not known where Wanda had moved to, so their only hope was that the post office knew. The minute they dropped the letter in the mail box they both felt happier and more care-free.

Days passed and there was no answer, but the letter did not come back so maybe Wanda had received it. Perhaps she was so hurt and angry she was not going to answer. You could not blame her. And Maddie remembered the way she hitched her left shoulder up as she walked off to school alone, and how the girls always said, "Why does her dress always hang funny like that, and why does she wear those queer, high, laced shoes?"

They knew she didn't have any mother, but they hadn't thought about it. They hadn't thought she had to do her own washing and ironing. She had only one dress and she must have had to wash and iron it overnight.

Maybe sometimes it wasn't dry when it was time to put it on in the morning. But it was always clean.

Several weeks went by and still Wanda did not answer. Peggy had begun to forget the whole business, and Maddie put herself to sleep at night making speeches about Wanda, defending her from great crowds of girls who were trying to tease her with, "How many dresses have you got?" Before Wanda could press her lips together in a tight line the way she did before answering, Maddie would cry out, "Stop! This girl is just a girl just like you are. . . ." And then everybody would feel ashamed the way she used to feel. Sometimes she rescued Wanda from a sinking ship or the hoofs of a runaway horse. "Oh, that's all right," she'd say when Wanda thanked her with dull pained eyes.

Now it was Christmas time and there was snow on the ground. Christmas bells and a small tree decorated the classroom. And on one narrow blackboard Jack Beggles had drawn a jolly fat Santa Claus in red and white chalk. On the last day of school before the holidays, the children in Peggy's and Maddie's class had a Christmas party. The teacher's desk was rolled back and a piano rolled in. First the children had acted the story of Tiny Tim. Then they had sung songs and Cecile had done some dances in different costumes. The dance called the "Passing of Autumn" in which she whirled and spun like a red and golden autumn leaf was the favorite.

After the party the teacher said she had a surprise, and she showed the class a letter she had received that morning.

"Guess who this is from," she said. "You remember Wanda Petronski? The bright little artist who won the draw-

"Peg!" she said. "Let me see your picture."

"What's the matter?" asked Peggy as they clattered up the stairs to her room, where Wanda's drawing was lying face down on the bed. Maddie carefully lifted it up.

"Look! She drew you. That's you!" she exclaimed. And the head and face of this picture did look like the auburn-haired Peggy.

"What did I say!" said Peggy. "She must have really liked us anyway."

"Yes, she must have," agreed Maddie, and she blinked away the tears that came every time she thought of Wanda standing alone in that sunny spot in the school yard close to the wall, looking stolidly over at the group of laughing girls after she had walked off, after she had said, "Sure, a hundred of them—all lined up . . ."

Eleanor Estes

A LETTER FROM
SANTA CLAUS

RUFUS WANTED A PONY. In this he was no different from every other small boy. Every Christmas Rufus asked Santa Claus for one. In his letters to Santa Claus, a pony always topped the list. Oh, of course, he used to ask for other things too, a bicycle, a top, an engine, toy soldiers, a jack-knife, but the pony was what he wanted more than anything else in the world. He tried in his letters to point this out to Santa Claus. For instance, in one letter he put a gold star by the word "pony." In another he wrote "pony" in red crayon. Still Santa Claus didn't seem to catch on, and he never brought a pony. He brought other fine things, pea blowers, horns, drums, and

Rufus was grateful for them but they didn't answer that longing he had inside for a pony.

How did he get it into his head he wanted a pony? Well, one day a couple of years ago, when the Moffats were living in the yellow house on New Dollar Street, a man had come along leading a black and white pony. You could have your picture taken sitting on its back for ten cents. Mama said Rufus should have one taken. She would frame it and put it on the mantel. So the man picked Rufus up and set him on the pony's back and took his picture. Then the man let Rufus ride the pony as far as Hughie Pudge's house. There, however, he had to get down and let Hughie Pudge get up, for he was going to have his picture taken too. Ever since that time when he had felt real pony flesh between his legs, Rufus had wanted a pony just terribly.

Last Christmas Santa Claus had brought him a brown felt pony on wheels, all right for very small children perhaps, but certainly not the thing for him. After this experience Rufus decided he'd better add the word "ALIVE" after "pony."

This Christmas Mama said to the children, "Do not ask Santa Claus for too much this year because, you know, there is a terrible war going on in Europe and Santa Claus will need an extra large amount of things for the Belgian children." So one evening, after the supper dishes had been cleared away, Jane and Rufus took pencil and paper to the kitchen table, pushed back the red-checked tablecloth and wrote their letters to Santa Claus.

Jane wrote:

> *Dear Santy Claus,*
> *Please bring me*
> *Two-storied pencil box*
> *Flexible flier sled*
> *Box of paints*
> *Princess and Curdie.*

Then she stopped for a moment. She would like to say, "Please don't bring any material for a dress or anything to wear, or for practical's sake." But perhaps Santa Claus would not think that was polite, so she signed,

> *With love,*
> *Jane Moffat.*

She looked over at Rufus' letter. "Have you finished?" she asked.

"Not quite," he answered. His tongue was between his teeth and he was working very hard.

Jane watched him curiously for he was no longer writing but was drawing something on his letter with brown crayon.

"How many things you ask for?" he demanded presently.

"Four," said Jane.

"Four!" repeated Rufus. "I only ast for one," he announced with satisfaction.

impatiently. "Because I don't have enough just by myself. And this brockated bag'll be from the whole three of us."

Rufus disappeared in the closet under the stairs and came back with his old Prince Albert tobacco box he kept his treasures in. Among the bottle tops in it he found a few pennies, six in all. He dropped them in Jane's lap.

Joe put his hand in his pocket. He kept his money there, when he had any, like a grown man. He pulled out two nickels and two pennies and dropped them in Jane's lap. Jane opened the little Chinese purse that Mama and Sylvie had brought her from New York's Chinatown. A nickel and four pennies fell out of this. Altogether it looked quite a pile. She scooped it up in the palm of her hand.

"Twenty-seven cents," she announced with satisfaction, shaking the coins up and down, up and down.

"Will that buy one of those bags?" asked Joe incredulously.

"Oh, no," replied Jane scornfully. "They cost a dollar at least. I'm goin' to make this brockated bag."

"Supposin' you don't finish it before Christmas?" asked Joe. "Then I'll have nothin' for Mama."

"I'll finish it," said Jane positively. Again she painted the bag she would make in glowing terms, for she saw that their enthusiasm was lagging. She rolled the words lovingly on her tongue, gold threads, silver threads, cerise, peacock blue, threads of silk and satin . . . brocaded . . . Well, they were won over again.

"Tomorrow we'll go to Aberdeen's and get the things," she concluded, exhausted from all this persuading, and putting all the coins in her purse.

The next day it was snowing very hard. It had begun in the middle of the night. Silently a soft, thick mantle had been laid over the earth and it was growing thicker by the minute. Jane and Joe and Rufus ran to the front window and looked out. Marvelous! The first deep snow of winter! They waved good-by to Sylvie who was making her way with difficulty through the deep drifts.

"Where's she goin'?" asked Rufus.

"To the Parish House to rehearse for the Christmas tableau," said Jane. "Come on. Get ready to go to Aberdeen's and get the things."

"All right, let's go," said Rufus impatiently.

They put on their rubbers. "Mine leak," said Jane, looking at the holes in the heels and toes. "But never mind, Santy Claus," she breathed, "I don't care a thing about whole rubbers." Rubbers would be worse to see on Christmas morning than material for a dress, she was thinking.

"Where are you going?" asked Mama.

Jane made grimaces at Rufus and Joe to keep them from saying, "Aberdeen's." This was to be a real surprise.

"We're just going out to play in the snow," said Jane carelessly.

"All right," said Mama, "but don't be gallivanting all over town. And come in when your feet get wet."

"All right. Good-by, Mama." And they each ran in to kiss her good-by, giving her a good hug besides. "Wait till she sees the brockated bag she's going to get," they thought.

Out into the snow they ran. The whole world was white. Soon they looked like snow men.

"Boy, oh, boy, I'll have plenty of shoveling to do when we get back," said Joe.

Although they could walk on the sidewalk, most of which had been cleared by the snow plow, they preferred to walk through the deep snow on the side of the pavements. They sank into the soft snow as far as their knees. This was good fun. After a while Jane said, "We better hurry. And anyway, my chilblains are itching me. And I want to get home and start that bag."

At last they reached Aberdeen's department store, the only large store in Cranbury. Rufus ran up to the show window and stretched his arms out wide. "Up to here is mine," he said, almost losing his balance. "And up to here is mine," laughed Jane, stretching her arms so wide she felt as though she would burst. It was still snowing so hard they could hardly see through the window. They did see that there was nothing there as pretty as the bag that Jane was going to make for Mama.

They pushed open the door. They sniffed the strange smells here, bolts of new material, rubber raincoats and overshoes, powder and perfumes. Because it was such a bad day, there were few people shopping. Joe, Jane, and Rufus stood at the goods counter and waited. Mrs. Aberdeen herself, dressed in many sweaters and a black apron, came to wait on them. She had a pencil stuck in the bun of her hair, a tape measure around her neck, and a pair of scissors strung on a black silk ribbon dangling from her bosom. Mrs. Aberdeen looked more like Madame-the-bust than anyone else in Cranbury.

"What do you want, children?" she asked briskly.

Jane looked at her, wondering how to begin. It was clear that Mrs. Aberdeen was not going to guess "brockated bag" just by looking at the three Moffats.

"Well, speak up," she said, more briskly still. "A spool of thread? A yard of elastic? Garters? Buttons?"

"No," said Jane. "We, that is, I, that is, we're all giving it, but I am making it, want to make a bag for Mama for Christmas."

"Oh, well . . . I see . . . well, now, how much money can you spend?"

Jane opened the little Chinese purse and the nickels and pennies rolled out on the counter.

"Twenty-seven cents," said Jane. "And I want to 'broider the bag."

"Yes. Well, twenty-seven cents won't buy much."

"A brockated bag," Jane breathed, but Mrs. Aberdeen didn't hear her.

"Here's a nice piece of goods you can have for that money," said Mrs. Aberdeen, holding up a piece of blue calico.

"I want to 'broider the bag," Jane repeated faintly.

Mrs. Aberdeen pulled out a skein of white embroidery cotton. "There," she said kindly. "I'm sure that will make a very nice bag."

"These things don't shine. Something is wrong," thought Jane, almost sobbing. But she paid the money and Mrs. Aberdeen deftly wrapped up the cloth and the embroidery thread in crackling green paper. With a real, bought package under her arm, Jane felt better. Then, too, the plain blue calico was out of sight and her vision of the brocaded bag returned in full force. It danced before her, a lovely elusive thing that quickened her pace. Joe and Rufus practically had to run to keep up with her.

"Will *that* be the brockated bag?" panted Joe.

"Wait and see," replied Jane with such an air of confidence that any doubts that Joe and Rufus might have had were cast immediately to the winds. By the time they reached home, the brocaded bag was again the beautiful teasing vision they all had had.

Mama was in the kitchen so they unwrapped the green package in the little green and white parlor with eager fingers. They would not have been surprised had the blue calico changed into a brocaded bag on the way home. However, the blue calico was still blue calico, though it was obvious from Jane's joyful spirits that she would have this transformed into the other lovely thing in no time.

During the next few days, Jane worked hard on the bag. She cut it out and sewed it up, every stitch by hand. She embroidered "MAMA" on one side of it with the white embroidery thread. On the other, she embroidered a daisy. When she finished it, she held it up and surveyed it with satisfaction. The brocaded bag! She saw it flash and sparkle and gleam with different shining colors. It was the very bag she had seen in the big store window in town.

In excitement she called Joe and Rufus in to see the finished bag. She dangled it before them, walked mincingly with it on her arm as elegant ladies do, thinking perhaps she looked like Mrs. Stokes.

"Is *that* a brockated bag?" they asked wonderingly.

"Yes!" said Jane. "Isn't it lovely?" And she walked up

to the mirror to look at herself with the pretty thing. Her eyes fell on the bag. What they saw there was a very plain blue calico bag with a crooked "MAMA" embroidered on one side and a humped-back daisy on the other. She looked down at the real bag hanging on her arm. The fair vision of the brocaded bag vanished completely and forever. She fell silent. The boys said nothing. After all, they had never seen a brocaded bag. In a while Jane said thoughtfully, "It will be good to keep buttons in."

They wrapped it up and made a card for it, "To Mama, with love from Joe, Rufus and Jane," and hid it where Mama would not be able to find it.

At last it was Christmas Eve. The four Moffats were making decorations for the tree, angels of gold and silver paper, baskets for candy and cookies, chains of colored paper, cornucopias for popcorn. The kitchen table was quite covered with scraps of paper and sticky with flour-and-water paste which Rufus had dabbed around by mistake. Sylvie had shown him how to make the chains of circles of bright paper. It was true that all of his chains were not linked together properly. His chain broke into short separate links that hung aimlessly from the whole. However, Sylvie said this did not matter in the slightest. Sylvie and Mama were going to help Santa Claus out by having the tree trimmed before he came late tonight. At present they were busy making the spiced Santa Claus cookies for the tree. How good they did smell!

"It is time now to hang your stockings," said Mama.

The four of them, even Sylvie, tore off to their rooms to find stockings that didn't have any holes in them so none of the good things would fall out of the heel or toe. They tacked these onto the wainscoting behind the kitchen stove, right handy for Santa Claus.

Now there was really nothing to do but go to bed. Rufus and Janey went first. They stripped off their clothes before the kitchen fire. They put on their outing flannel bed-socks and nightclothes and raced noisily up the stairs to bed.

But not to sleep! Not yet! They talked and laughed, smothering their giggles under the bedclothes. They whispered, "What do you think Santy Claus will bring us?"

"Let's stay awake all night and watch for Santy Claus," said Rufus.

"What are Mama and Sylvie so mysterious about?" Jane asked.

"What do you think Santy will bring?" Rufus asked this for the hundredth time, although there was really little doubt in his mind. Had he not written Santa Claus the same letter every night for a week, telling him to bring a real live pony, even showing by drawings exactly what he meant? Goodness knows how many of these letters had found their way to Santa Claus. So many probably that Rufus had grown rather worried at the last and varied his letter to read,

> DEAR SANTY,
>   *Please bring me a live pony. ONE*
> *is plenty.*
>   RUFUS.

"Goodness," he chuckled, "if Santy brought a pony for every letter I wrote! . . . But I guess he'll know better than that."

In spite of themselves, they began to grow sleepy. Then Joe came to bed and talked for a while, but soon Joey and Rufus became quiet and Jane knew they were asleep. Jane stayed awake, however. Her chilblains itched her. But she wasn't thinking about them so much. She was thinking about Rufus and that pony he expected.

"He certainly does want that pony," she thought. "He wants that pony harder than I have ever wanted anything."

And this year he was so positive that Santa would bring one. Nevertheless, Jane had a sinking feeling in her stomach that Christmas morning would come and there just would not be a pony for Rufus. What should she do? His disappointment would be more than she could bear. "Something oughter be done," she worried, "but what?"

Just then Sylvie came upstairs and climbed into bed.

"Asleep, Janekin?" she asked softly.

Jane didn't answer, pretending to be asleep. There was no use troubling Sylvie about this pony business too. After a while she could tell from Sylvie's breathing that she was asleep. For a long time Jane lay there. Supposing she stayed awake this year and listened for Santa Claus? A word in his ear about the pony might work wonders. Other years she had meant to do this, but somehow morning had always come and the stockings had been filled as by magic and she would realize that she had gone to sleep and missed Santa Claus after all. He had come in the middle of the night.

This year would be different though. She would stay awake
—yes, she would.

She listened to all the night noises: the frost making
the windowpanes creak; Mama calling Catherine-the-cat;
Mama turning the key in the latch, winding the clock, shaking down the kitchen fire and the fire in the parlor. Finally
she heard Mama drop first one shoe and then the other
with a soft thud to the floor, and she knew that Mama too
was in bed.

Now all she had to do was to listen for Santa Claus.
Surely he would be here soon. It must be very late—midnight, probably. She would stay awake and stay awake.
. . . She would say to him, "Please, Santy, a pony for Rufus. . . ." The first thing she would hear would be the
sleighbells and the reindeer's hooves on the roof. . . . She
must stay awake and . . .

In telling Nancy about this night later, Jane was positive she had stayed awake. Positive that just as the clock in
the sitting room downstairs struck twelve, Santa Claus had
stood beside her bed and gently turned her over. His frosty
beard had even brushed her cheek. And he had whispered
something in her ear. But just as she was about to speak to
him, he had vanished and the sleighbells tinkled off in the
distance.

She sat up in bed. Sylvie was sleeping peacefully. Santa
Claus had gone. Of that she was sure. Oh, why had he not
waited for her to speak? Softly she crept out of bed, felt her
way past the chiffonier into the hall, and stole down the
creaking stairs to the kitchen. She was grateful for the faint
light that shone from the kitchen stove. Finding the

matches, she struck one. Catherine-the-cat's eyes shone green and examined her with keen disapproval. Paying no attention to her, Jane glanced swiftly behind the stove. There the four stockings hung, bulging now. Yes, that proved it. Santa had been here just now and had come to her side to give her some message.

She glanced around the room and peeked into the little parlor where the Christmas tree was shining. There was no pony about. That was certain. She tiptoed to the back window and pressed her face against the pane. The moon shone over the white snow, making a light almost as bright as day. If there had been a pony out there, she would know it. There just wasn't any pony and there was no use hoping for it any longer. That was why Santa had come to her bedside. He knew she was awake and waiting and he had a good reason for not bringing the pony, and that's what he had wanted to tell her. What was the reason? She thought for a moment. Then she knew. She lighted another match, found a piece of brown wrapping paper and a pencil. Crouching on the floor near the stove she wrote,

> Dear Rufus,
> All the ponies are at the war.
> Your friend,
> Santy Claus.

She tucked this note in the top of Rufus' stocking and went back to bed. Shivering, she pressed her cold self against Sylvie and fell sound asleep.

The next thing she knew, Sylvie was shaking her and

shaking her and screaming, "Merry Christmas, Merry Christmas!" Jane jumped out of bed, pulled a blanket around her, danced wildly out of the room screaming, "Merry Christmas, Merry Christmas!" Mama gave them each a sweet hug and a kiss and said, "Merry Christmas, everybody." The whole house echoed and Catherine-the-cat chased her tail for the first time in five and a half years.

They grabbed their stockings and raced back to bed with them, for the house was still bitterly cold. A sudden yell from Rufus interrupted everything.

"Whoops!" he shouted. "Whoops! Listen to this! Mama! Listen! I've had a letter from Santy Claus."

Rufus jumped out of bed and tore through the house like a cyclone, the others following him.

"Listen to this," he said again, when they were finally collected before the kitchen fire. " 'Dear Rufus,' it says. 'Dear Rufus, All the ponies are at the war,' and it's signed 'Your friend, Santy Claus!' Imagine a letter from Santy Claus himself!"

Mama put on her glasses and examined the note carefully.

"H-m-m-m," she said.

"Gee," said Rufus, "wait till I show this to Eddie Bangs. He's always boastin' of his autograps collection. He's got President Taft, Mayor Harley, Chief Mulligan. But he ain't got Santy Claus."

Jane could see that having a letter from Santa Claus himself softened considerably Rufus' disappointment in not getting a real live pony.

When calm was somewhat restored, the gifts were

taken from the tree. These were some of the most exciting moments: When Mama opened her "brockated bag" and said, "This will be elegant to keep buttons in"; when Rufus opened his toy village—houses, trees, grocery boys on bicycles, delivery men with horses and wagons, firemen and fire engines, a postman, a policeman and a milkman—yes, a complete village to lay out with streets and parks; when Jane opened her miniature grocery store, with tiny boxes of real cocoa and salt, sacks of sugar and the smallest jars of real honey; when Sylvie opened a huge box and drew out a fluffy white dress Mama had secretly made for her first ball, the Junior-Senior promenade; and when Joe opened a long, slim package that had a shining clarinet in it! "Boy, oh, boy," was all he could say.

But now it was time for Sylvie to go to church to take her part in the Christmas tableau. Of course all the Moffats were going to watch her and join in the beautiful Christmas carols. Before they left, however, Mama gathered them all around the tree and they sang:

> "Hark! The herald angels sing
> Glory to the newborn King.
> Peace on earth and mercy mild
> God and sinners reconciled!"

E. L. Konigsburg

ELIOT MILES DOES NOT WISH YOU A MERRY CHRISTMAS BECAUSE . . .

LIOT MILES was born at 10:09 P.M. on Christmas Eve. He knew that he would be granted any wish he made at exactly that moment every night before Christmas if he crossed his fingers, shut his eyes (tight!), lay flat on his back and was truly serious. Last year, when he was eight, he had wished for a new bike; he got it, even though it was the wrong color. When he was seven he had wished for a trip to Disneyland; he got it, even though the whole family, including his brother Harold, had come along. Each year something had been a little wrong.

On this Christmas morning, the first morning of his ninth year, he walked past the tree in the living room into the kitchen, where Harold was eating breakfast. Harold asked him what he had wished for this year, and Eliot told him that it was nothing that could be wrapped and put under a tree. Harold asked what it was and Eliot told him. He had wished never to be wrong ever again.

Harold held the cereal box under the table and challenged Eliot to tell him how many ounces in the box. Eliot said that he didn't know and that Harold ought to understand the difference between never being wrong and knowing everything. Harold said he didn't understand, and Eliot gave him this example:

"Let's say that Mom tells me to wear my raincoat, and I say, 'No,' and she says, 'You're going to get wet on the way home,' and I say, 'No, *I won't.*' Well, I won't."

"Won't what?"

"Get wet."

"Okay, smarty, then tell me if it's going to rain today."

Eliot explained that he hadn't wished to be a fortune-teller either. He had just wished never to be wrong ever again.

At that moment Mrs. Miles came into the kitchen and told Eliot that she had been waiting in the living room for him to open his presents and that he had better open Grandma's gift before she arrived. Eliot told his mother that he had plenty of time to open Grandma's gift. When Mrs. Miles asked Eliot how he knew that, he told her that he never was going to be wrong ever again. Mrs. Miles told Eliot that she thought his Christmas spirit was awful and she never knew such an ungrateful child.

Then Mr. Miles came into the kitchen. He wanted to know what Eliot had done to upset Mrs. Miles, and why didn't Eliot open his present from Grandma before she came, and why didn't he take out the dog before the dog had an accident. Eliot told his father that he had plenty of time to open Grandma's gift and that the dog would not have an accident. When Mr. Miles asked him how he knew so much, he told his father that he never was going to be wrong ever again. Mr. Miles told Eliot that he'd better open the present *now* and take the dog out *now* because if he didn't, he was going to have an accident even if the dog did not, that his backside was going to collide with the palm of his father's hand.

Eliot opened the present and Eliot took out the dog.

Eliot was furious—with Harold, with his mother, with his father, with the dog, with Christmas. In short, he was mad at himself; he should have wished never to be wrong ever again *and* to have everyone believe him. What good was a Christmas wish that would allow him to be wrong at the very moment (10:09 P.M.) he was wishing never to be wrong ever again?

Madeleine L'Engle

A FULL HOUSE

TO ANYBODY who lives in a city or even a sizable town, it may not sound like much to be the director of a volunteer choir in a postcard church in a postcard village, but I was the choir director and largely responsible for the Christmas Eve service, so it was very much of a much for me. I settled my four children and my father, who was with us for Christmas, in a front pew and went up to the stuffy choir-robing room. I was missing my best baritone, my husband, Wally, because he had been called to the hospital. He's a country doctor, and I'm used to his pocket beeper going off during the church service. I missed him, of course, but I knew he'd been called to deliver a baby, and a Christmas baby is always a joy.

The service went beautifully. Nobody flatted, and Eugenia Underhill, my lead soprano, managed for once not to breathe in the middle of a word. The only near disaster came when she reached for the high C in "O Holy Night," hit it brilliantly—and then down fell her upper plate. Eugenia took it in good stride, pushed her teeth back in place and finished her solo. When she sat down, she doubled over with mirth.

The church looked lovely, lighted entirely by candlelight, with pine boughs and holly banking the windows. The Christmas Eve service is almost entirely music, hence my concern; there is never a sermon, but our minister reads excerpts from the Christmas sermons of John Donne and Martin Luther.

When the dismissal and blessing were over, I heaved a sigh of relief. Now I could attend to our own Christmas at home. I collected my family, and we went out into the night. A soft, feathery snow was beginning to fall. People called out "Good-night" and "Merry Christmas." I was happily tired, and ready for some peace and quiet for the rest of the evening—our service is over by nine.

I hitched Rob, my sleeping youngest, from one hip to the other. The two girls, Vicky and Suzy, walked on either side of their grandfather; John, my eldest, was with me. They had all promised to go to bed without protest as soon as we had finished all our traditional Christmas rituals. We seem to add new ones each year so that Christmas-Eve bedtime gets later and later.

I piled the kids into the station wagon, thrusting Rob into John's arms. Father and I got in the front, and I drove off into the snow, which was falling more heavily. I hoped that it would not be a blizzard and that Wally would get home before the roads got too bad.

Our house is on the crest of a hill, a mile out of the village. As I looked uphill, I could see the lights of our outdoor Christmas tree twinkling warmly through the snow. I turned up our back road, feeling suddenly very tired. When I drove up to the garage and saw that Wally's car was not there, I tried not to let Father or the children see my disappointment. I began ejecting the kids from the back. It was my father who first noticed what looked like a bundle of clothes by the storm door.

"Victoria," he called to me. "What's this?"

The bundle of clothes moved. A tear-stained face emerged, and I recognized Evie, who had moved from the village with her parents two years ago, when she was 16. She had been our favorite and most loyal baby-sitter, and we all missed her. I hadn't seen her—or heard anything about her—in all this time.

"Evie!" I cried. "What is it? What's the matter?"

She moved stiffly, as though she had been huddled there in the cold for a long time. Then she held her arms out to me in a childlike gesture. "Mrs. Austin—" She sighed as I bent down to kiss her. And then, "Mom threw me out. So I came here." She dropped the words simply, as though she had no doubt that she would find a welcome in our home. She had on a shapeless, inadequate coat, and a bare toe stuck through a hole in one of her sneakers.

I put my arms around her and helped her up. "Come in. You must be frozen."

The children were delighted to see Evie and crowded around, hugging her, so it was a few minutes before we got into the kitchen and past the dogs who were loudly welcoming us home. There were Mr. Rochester, our Great Dane; Colette, a silver-gray French Poodle who bossed the big dog unmercifully; and, visiting us for the Christmas holidays while his owners were on vacation, a ten-month-old Manchester terrier named Guardian. Daffodil, our fluffy amber cat, jumped on top of the fridge to get out of the way, and Prune Whip, our black-and-white cat, skittered across the floor and into the living room.

The kids turned on lights all over downstairs, and John called, "Can I turn on the Christmas-tree lights?"

"Sure," I answered, "but light the fire first."

I turned again to Evie, who simply stood in the middle of the big kitchen-dining room, not moving. "Evie, welcome. I'm sorry it's such chaos—let me take your coat." At first she resisted and then let me slip the worn material off her shoulders. Under the coat she wore a sweater and a plaid skirt; the skirt did not button, but was fastened with a pin, and for an obvious reason: Evie was not about to produce another Christmas baby, but she was very definitely pregnant.

Her eyes followed mine. Rather defiantly, she said, "That's why I'm here."

I thought of Evie's indifferent parents, and I thought about Christmas Eve. I put my arm around her for a gentle hug. "Tell me about it."

"Do I have to?"

"I think it might help, Evie."

anyone else. When he said that, I knew it was his way of telling me to get out, just like Mom and Pop."

The girls had wandered back into the kitchen while we were talking, and Suzy jogged at my elbow. "Why does Evie's tummy look so big?"

The phone rang. I called, "John, get it, please."

In a moment he came into the kitchen, looking slightly baffled. "It was someone from the hospital saying Dad's on his way home, and would we please make up the bed in the waiting room."

Evie looked up from her soup. "Mrs. Austin—" She turned her frightened face toward me, fearful, no doubt, that we were going to put her out.

"It's all right, Evie." I was thinking quickly. "John, would you mind sleeping in the guest room with Grandfather?"

"If Grandfather doesn't mind."

My father called from the living room, "Grandfather would enjoy John's company."

"All right then, Evie." I poured more soup into her bowl. "You can sleep in John's bed. Rob will love sharing his room with you."

"But who is Daddy bringing home?" John asked.

"What's wrong with Evie's tummy?" Suzy persisted.

"And why didn't Daddy tell us?" Vicky asked.

"Tell us what?" Suzy demanded.

"Who he's bringing home with him!" John said.

Evie continued to spoon soup into her mouth, at the same time struggling not to cry. I put one hand on her shoulder, and she reached up for it, asking softly, as the girls and John went into the living room, "Mrs. Austin, I knew you wouldn't turn me out on Christmas Eve, but what about . . . well, may I stay with you for a little while? I have some thinking to do."

"Of course you can, and you do have a lot of thinking to do—the future of your baby, for instance."

"I know. Now that it's getting so close, I'm beginning to get really scared. At first I thought I wanted the baby, I thought it would make Billy and me closer, make us a family like you and Dr. Austin and your kids, but now I know that was just wishful thinking. Sometimes I wish I could go back, be your baby-sitter again . . . Mrs. Austin, I just don't know what I'm going to do with a baby of my own."

I pressed her hand. "Evie, I know how you feel, but things have a way of working out. Try to stop worrying, at least tonight—it's Christmas Eve."

"And I'm home," Evie said. "I feel more at home in this house than anywhere else."

I thought of my own children and hoped that they would never have cause to say that about someone else's house. To Evie I said, "Relax then, and enjoy Christmas. The decisions don't have to be made tonight."

My father ambled into the kitchen, followed by the three dogs. "I think the dogs are telling me they need to go out," he said. "I'll just walk around the house with them and see what the night is doing." He opened the kitchen door and let the dogs precede him.

I opened the curtains, not only to watch the progress of my father and the dogs, but to give myself a chance to think about Evie and how we could help her. More was needed, I knew, than just a few days' shelter. She had no money, no home, and a baby was on the way. . . . No wonder she looked scared—and trapped. I watched the falling snow and longed to hear the sound of my husband's car. Like Vicky, I wondered who on earth he was bringing home with him. Then I saw headlights coming up the road and heard a car slowing down, but the sound was not the slightly bronchial purr of Wally's car. Before I had a chance to wonder who it could be, the phone rang. "I'll get it!" Suzy yelled, and ran, beating Vicky. "Mother, it's Mrs. Underhill."

I went to the phone. Eugenia's voice came happily over the line. "Wasn't the Christmas Eve service beautiful! And did you see my teeth?" She laughed.

"You sang superbly, anyhow."

"Listen, why I called—you have two ovens, don't you?"

"Yes."

"Something's happened to mine. The burners work, but the oven is dead, and there's no way I can get anyone to fix it now. So what I wondered is, can I cook my turkey in one of your ovens?"

"Sure," I said, though I'd expected to use the second oven for the creamed-onion casserole and sweet potatoes—but how could I say no to Eugenia?

"Can I come over with my turkey now?" she asked. "I like to put it in a slow oven Christmas Eve, the way you taught me. Then I won't have to bother you again till tomorrow."

"Sure, Eugenia, come on over, but drive carefully."

"I will. Thanks," she said.

John murmured, "Just a typical Christmas Eve at the Austins'," as the kitchen door opened, and my father and the dogs came bursting in, followed by a uniformed state trooper.

When Evie saw him, she looked scared.

My father introduced the trooper, who turned to me. "Mrs. Austin, I've been talking with your father here, and I think we've more or less sorted things out." Then he looked at Evie. "Young lady, we've been looking for you. We want to talk to you about your friends."

The color drained from her face.

"Don't be afraid," the trooper reassured her. "We just want to know where we can find you. I understand that you'll be staying with the Austins for a while—for the next few weeks, at least." He looked at my father, who nodded, and I wondered what the two had said to each other. Was Evie in more trouble than I thought?

She murmured something inaudible, keeping her eyes fastened to her soup.

"Well, now, it's Christmas Eve," the trooper said, "and I'd like to be getting on home. It's bedtime for us all."

"We're waiting for Daddy," Suzy said. "He's on his way home."

"And he's bringing someone with him," Vicky added.

"Looks like you've got a full house," the trooper said. "Well, 'night, folks."

My father showed him out, then shut the door behind him.

"What was that—" John started to ask.

I quickly said, "What I want all of you to do is to go upstairs, right now, and get ready for bed. That's an order."

"But what about Daddy—"

"And whoever he's bringing—"

"And reading 'The Night Before Christmas' and Saint Luke—"

"And you haven't sung to us—"

I spoke through the clamor. "Upstairs. Now. You can come back down as soon as you're all ready for bed."

Evie rose. "Shall I get Rob?" I had the feeling she wanted to get away, escape my questions.

"We might as well leave him. Vicky, get Evie some nightclothes from my closet, please."

When they had all finally trooped upstairs, including Evie, I turned to my father who was perched on a stool by the kitchen counter. "All right, Dad, tell me about it," I said. "What did the officer tell you?"

"That soup smells mighty good," he said. I filled a bowl for him and waited.

Finally he said, "Evie was going with a bunch of kids who weren't much good. A couple of them were on drugs— not Evie, fortunately, or her boyfriend. And they stole some cars, just for kicks, and then abandoned them. The police are pretty sure that Evie wasn't involved, but they want to talk to her and her friends, and they've been trying to round them up. They went to her parents' house looking for her. Her mother and father made it seem as if she'd run away—they didn't mention that they'd put her out. All they did was denounce her, but they did suggest she might have come here."

"Poor Evie. There's so much good in her, and sometimes I wonder how, with her background. What did you tell the trooper?"

"I told him Evie was going to stay with you and Wally for the time being, that you would take responsibility for her. They still want to talk to her, but I convinced him to wait until after Christmas. I guess the trooper figured that, as long as she's with you, she would be looked after and out of harm's way."

"Thank goodness. All she needs is to be hauled into a station house on Christmas Eve—" Just then the heavy knocker on the kitchen door banged.

It was Eugenia, with a large turkey in a roasting pan in her arms. "I'll just pop it in the oven," she said. "If you think about basting it when you baste yours, okay, but it'll do all right by itself. Hey, you don't have yours in yet!"

What with one thing and another, I'd forgotten our turkey, but it was prepared and ready in the cold pantry. I whipped out and brought it in and put it in the other oven.

As Eugenia drove off, the dogs started with their welcoming bark, and I heard the sound of Wally's engine.

The children heard, too, and came rushing downstairs. "Wait!" I ordered. "Don't mob Daddy. And remember he has someone with him."

Evie came slowly downstairs, wrapped in an old blue plaid robe of mine. John opened the kitchen door, and the dogs went galloping out.

"Whoa! Down!" I could hear my husband command.

And then, to the children, "Make way!" The children scattered, and Wally came in, his arm around a young woman whom I had never seen before. She was holding a baby in her arms.

"This is Maria Heraldo," Wally said. "Maria, my wife, Victoria. And—" He looked at the infant.

"Pepita," she said, "after her father."

Wally took the babe. "Take off your coat," he said to the mother. "Maria's husband was killed in an accident at work two weeks ago. Her family are all in South America, and she was due to be released from the hospital today. Christmas Eve didn't seem to me to be a very good time for her to be alone."

I looked at the baby, who had an amazing head of dark hair. "She isn't the baby—"

"That I delivered tonight? No, though that little boy was slow in coming—that's why we're so late." He smiled down at the young woman. "Pepita was born a week ago." He looked up and saw our children hovering in the doorway, Evie and my father behind them. When he saw Evie, he raised his eyebrows in a questioning gesture.

"Evie's going to be staying with us for a while," I told him. Explanations would come later. "Maria, would you like some soup?"

"I would," my husband said, "and Maria will have some, too." He glanced at the children. "Vicky and Suzy, will you go up to the attic, please, and bring down the cradle?"

They were off like a flash.

My husband questioned the young mother. "Tired?"

"No. I slept while the little boy was being delivered. So did Pepita." And she looked with radiant pride at her daughter who was sleeping again.

"Then let's all go into the living room and warm ourselves in front of the fire. We have some Christmas traditions you might like to share with us."

The young woman gazed up at him, at me, "I'm so grateful to you—"

"Nonsense. Come along."

Then Maria saw Evie, and I watched her eyes flick to Evie's belly, then upward, and the two young women exchanged a long look. Evie's glance shifted to the sleeping child, and then she held out her arms. Maria gently handed her the baby, and Evie took the child and cradled it in her arms. For the first time that evening a look of peace seemed to settle over her features.

It is not easy for a woman to raise a child alone, and Maria would probably go back to her family. In any case, her child had obviously been conceived in love, and even death could not take that away. Evie's eyes were full of tears as she carried Pepita into the living room, but she no longer looked so lost and afraid, and I had the feeling that whatever happened, Evie would be able to handle it. She would have our help—Wally's and mine—for as long as she needed it, but something told me that she wouldn't need it for long.

In a short while, Maria was ensconced in one of the big chairs, a bowl of soup on the table beside her. Evie put the baby in the cradle, and knelt, rocking it gently. Wally sat on the small sofa with Rob in his lap, a mug of soup in

one hand. The two girls were curled up on the big daven-
port, one on either side of their grandfather, who had his
arms around them. I sat across from Maria, and Evie came
and sat on the footstool by me. John was on the floor in
front of the fire. The only light was from the Christmas tree
and the flickering flames of the fire. On the mantel were a
cup of cocoa and a plate of cookies.

"Now," my husband said, " 'Twas the night before
Christmas, when all through the house . . .' "

When he had finished, with much applause from the
children and Evie and Maria, he looked to me. "Your
turn."

John jumped up and handed me my guitar. I played
and sang, "I Wonder as I Wander," and then "In the Bleak
Midwinter," and ended up with "Let All Mortal Flesh Keep
Silence." As I put the guitar away, I saw Maria reach out
for Evie, and the two of them briefly clasped hands.

"And now," Wally said, "your turn, please, Grandfather."

My father opened his Bible and began to read. When
he came to, "And she brought forth her firstborn son, and
wrapped him in swaddling clothes, and laid him in a manger; because there was no room for them in the inn," I
looked at Maria, who was rocking the cradle with her foot
while her baby murmured in her sleep. Evie, barely turning,
keeping her eyes fastened on the sleeping infant, leaned her
head against my knee, rubbing her cheek against the wool
of my skirt.

Suzy was sleeping with her head down in her grandfather's lap, while he continued to read: "And suddenly there

was with the angel a multitude of the heavenly host praising God, and saying, Glory to God in the highest, and on earth peace, good will toward men."

I remembered John saying, "Just a typical Christmas Eve at the Austins'," and I wondered if there ever could be such a thing as a typical Christmas. For me, each one is unique. This year our house was blessed by Evie and her unborn child, by Eugenia's feeling free to come and put her turkey in our stove, and by Maria and Pepita turning our plain New England farmhouse into a stable.

Elizabeth Yates

ONCE IN THE YEAR

WHEN SUPPER WAS OVER, Martha and Andrew put on their warm coats. Andrew pulled his cap down over his ears and Martha threw a woolen shawl over her head and tied it under her chin. Laughter was in their voices and lightness in their movements, for this was one time when care could be set aside. The animals had been fed early and bedded down for the night so that Andrew had no worries for them; and Martha had spent the whole week cooking and cleaning so her mind was free from household chores. Her husband and her son, and Benj who had been part of the farm for so many years, would not want for anything that was hers to give them for days to come.

"You'll be asleep when we get back," Andrew said, just as they were going out the door, "so the next greeting we'll be giving you will be Merry Christmas."

Martha's eyes twinkled. Even the plain words said every night of the year, "Good-night, Peter," seemed so much more meaningful when the next ones would be "Merry Christmas!"

Then they called good-by and stepped out into the frosty night.

Peter ran to the window and pushed the curtain aside to watch them. Arm in arm they went over the path, two black figures on the white field of snow, with stars looking down on them and the dark lines of the hills rimming them in a known world. Now they were running a little, then they stopped as if to catch their breath and Peter saw his mother toss her head quickly, then his father threw back his head and laughed.

What a wonderful time Christmas Eve was, Peter thought, the world so still and everyone in it so happy. For so many days of the year his father was serious and full of care and his mother's thoughts seemed far ahead of her as if she were thinking of all the things she had to do; but tonight they were gay and lighthearted.

When Peter could see them no longer, he returned to the circle of warmth by the stove. Benj was sitting there, gazing dreamily into the coals. Peter brought up a stool and sat beside him. It might be beautiful outside and great things might be going on in the village, but here it was warm and the deep wonder of the night was as much within the familiar kitchen as it was outdoors in the starlit quiet.

"Tell me a story, Benj. Tell me about Christmas, how it all happened," Peter said.

Peter knew it well but he wanted to hear it again, and though the story itself did not change, Benj never failed to add something new at the end.

Benj nodded slowly and began to tell Peter the old story of the stable at Bethlehem, of the man and woman who had found shelter there because there was no room at the inn, and of the ox and the ass who had moved aside a little to share their place with the travelers.

"And out on the hillside there were shepherds with their sheep," Benj went on, "some of them talking around a bit of a fire they had made, holding out their hands to warm them for there was a chill on the air that night; and some of them had gone to sleep. But, of a sudden, the night about them became white with light. They looked up to see where the light came from and it was as if the very doors of heaven had opened to them. Then they heard an angel telling them what had happened."

"What had happened, Benj? What made the night turn to light?"

"In that stable yonder in Bethlehem a child had been born to the woman. He it was that the ages had been waiting for. He it was who would bring true light to the world, and though he would not do it as a child, nor yet as a young man, and though the world would stumble on in its darkness for many years until he came to the fullness of his manhood, there was light that night of his birth. A kind of sign it was of what his coming into the world meant, and the darkness would never be so dark again."

Benj was seeing it all, as clearly as had the shepherds on that far away hillside, and his eyes were shining.

"The shepherds left their flocks in charge of their dogs and went to the stable to see the child. A fine strong boy he was. They brought food in their pouches to share with the man and the woman, and when they returned to the hillside they were not hungry, for the joy they bore with them fed them as heartily as the bread and the cheese they had left behind. After a while the night grew quiet again. Midnight came. The family were alone in the stable. And then —" Benj breathed deeply, as if recalling something so marvelous that there might not be words to tell of it, "a wonderful thing happened."

"What was it, Benj?" Peter asked. The story had been familiar to him up to this point but now it was new.

"In that dark stillness, unbroken by even a baby's crying, the creatures in the stable began to talk among themselves—the great slow-moving ox, and the tired little ass, a half-grown sheep that had followed the shepherds to Bethlehem, and a brown hen who had roosted in the rafters at sundown. They talked together and to the child."

"Didn't they talk to the others—the man and the woman?"

Benj shook his head. "Those two had gone to sleep." He looked at Peter and spoke slowly. "It's said that on every Christmas Eve, near midnight and for a while after, the creatures talk among themselves. It is the only time they do so, the only time of all the year."

"Can anyone hear them, Benj?"

The old man shook his head again. "Only the still of

heart, for only they will listen long enough to catch the meaning of so strange a sound."

"Have you heard them, Benj?"

"I have, Peter, times without number, and they always say the same thing."

"What do they say?"

"I cannot tell you now. What they say to me might be very different from what they would say to anyone else."

Peter looked at the clock. The hands were at nine. Such a long way it was to midnight, yet he knew that somehow he must stay awake to hear the creatures talk together.

A while later Benj banked the stove, lowered the lamp and said good-night to Peter. Peter went upstairs to bed and Benj went out to the barn to make his nightly rounds. The animals were safe and contented, he knew, but this was one night when he must be doubly sure, tired though his limbs might be from the work of the day.

The quietness of night enveloped the farmhouse, enveloped the world; but the night was unlike any other, for wonder was abroad and there was an air of expectancy that beggared sleep.

Up in his room, Peter heard the clock strike eleven, then he heard the laughter of his mother and the well-known tones of his father's voice as they came up the path from the village. Their voices lowered as they entered the house and talked together in the kitchen, warming their hands by the stove. Quietly they came up the stairs and stood outside Peter's door, then the door was pushed open a crack.

"He's asleep," Andrew said.

"Good, then we haven't wakened him," Martha added. She would have liked to cross the room and tuck his covers in, but she would not risk waking him at such an hour and the next day Christmas.

Peter lay very still, his eyelids trembling as he kept them closed over his eyes. What would his mother say if she came over to the bed and saw that he had not undressed— that he had put a stone under his pillow so discomfort would keep him awake? The door closed and his parents tiptoed into their own room. There were small sounds and whispers, a bit of soft laughter, then stillness and the ticking of the kitchen clock telling Peter that its hands were drawing near midnight.

Slowly, one foot then another, he got out of bed and put on his coat that had been made from the wool of Biddy's last shearing. He took his shoes in his hands and crept down the stairs to the kitchen. Peering up into the face of the clock he saw the hands at a quarter to twelve. He sat down on the floor to put on his shoes. Going to the door he opened it noiselessly and closed it behind him, then ran lightly to the barn.

It was very still in the barn and very dark, but as his eyes became used to the darkness he could discern dimly the familiar shapes of the farm animals in their chosen positions of sleep. The barn seemed strange so near the mid hour of night and Peter, to assure himself, went to each animal in turn, to caress them and feel the comfort of their knowing presences.

First, there was the black yearling, Biddy's last lamb, who was growing to be the flock's leader. Peter slipped into the pen where the sheep were folded and whistled softly. The yearling shook itself out of sleep and came over to the boy, rubbing against him and eating the raw potato Peter had brought in his pocket.

Then Peter went to the stall where his father's work horse stood. The horse whinnied and reached for the lump of sugar Peter offered.

Then he went to the stanchions where the cows were, all three of them lying with their legs tucked under them and chewing their cuds peacefully. Peter stroked each gentle head and took the rhythmic sound of chewing as their sufficient greeting.

Going over to the corner where the hens roosted for the night, he looked up at them.

"Hello," he said. "It's just Peter. Don't be alarmed."

They moved on their perch ever so lightly and started talking among themselves, soft sounds as if they were so far asleep they could bear to be wakened but still must let Peter know that they were aware of his presence and were glad for it.

Peter found a pile of hay near the horse's stall and curled up in it to listen to the creatures when midnight came. He was hardly settled when from far down in the valley the village clock could be heard. Peter held his breath as twelve strokes resounded on the night with slow and measured import. While their echo faded, the same stillness filled the barn that had been there when Peter first entered; but it was only for a moment. Soon it was broken by a rustle of straw here, and a stamp of a hoof there, a single deep-toned baa-aa, a short neigh, and chickens cooing in their sleep.

Almost before Peter realized what had happened, he was caught up in a conversation the creatures were having. It was an old story they were telling, as far as he could make out, one the horse had heard as a colt from his dam, and long before that it had first been told by a small weary ass. It was a story the cow had heard as a calf and which had been first told by an ox in a stable in Judea. It was a story that the sheep knew because all sheep heard it from their ewes when they were lambs. It was a story that a single brown hen had left as a heritage for all hens. And they told it again, each in a way peculiar to cow, horse, sheep, hen, as if to remind themselves of why this night was hallowed.

"I had worked all day," the cow said, thinking for that moment that she was the ox and might speak as such. "I had drawn heavy loads and knocked my feet against the rough stones in the fields, but when the child was born and all that light shone in my stable the work I had done seemed a beautiful thing and the thought of it no longer tired me. It was the light that made me see we were born to serve so One on high might rule."

"Oh, I was weary, too," the horse said, and his voice became small and plaintive as he fancied himself the ass. "We had journeyed so far that day, so very far, and mind you, as it turned out, it was two I had been carrying, not just one. My head drooped so low that I thought I could never lift it again and even the hay in the manger did not interest me. Then came that light and everything was differ-ent. I felt so humble in its glow that I did not care if I never raised my head again. And I was glad my back was strong to bear burdens and that my feet could be sure, no matter how rough the way. I was glad, too, that man had use for me, for serving him brought me closer to the God he serves."

"I was not weary or burdened," the black yearling spoke up, thinking he was the half-grown lamb that had followed in the wake of the shepherds. "I had been grazing all day and when darkness came and the flock had been folded I had tucked my legs under me to sleep. Then the light appeared. It was such a dazzling thing it took away from me all thinking. There were no thoughts in my head, such as 'Shall I stay? Shall I go?' There was only one compelling desire and it drew me to the stable where I stayed. I saw my shepherd giving his pouch of food to the mother and I thought then, 'Take what I have and use it, it is all for glory.' "

One of the hens shook her feathers and came down from the roost. The sound of her voice was sweetly melodious, as if the feathered creatures of the world in making her their spokesman had loaned her the gift of song.

"I said to myself, 'This is a very great moment. How shall I praise God for letting me be here?' There was only one thing to do. I nestled down in the straw and laid an egg so when it came time for the night's fast to be broken there would be something for hungry folk to eat. And so, ever since that time long ago, an egg has been our way of praise. It is our highest gift."

The rustling in the straw ceased. The hen's slow sleepy movements on the roost were over. Not so much as the stamp of a hoof or the muffled baa-ing of a sheep broke the stillness in the barn. Peter rubbed his eyes in astonishment. He had heard the creatures talking on Christmas Eve, talking of what had taken place on the first Christmas Eve.

He knew something now of what dwelt behind the quietness in the soft eyes of horse and cow, the gentle gaze of the sheep, and the cool glance of the hen. They had never forgotten the time when they had been of use, and remembering it had marked their lives with blessing. Like a shining thread running down the ages, it gave meaning and dignity to the work each one did. Love had made them wise that night, lightening every labor they might do thereafter.

There was a stir among the dark shadows of the barn and Peter saw old Benj coming to stand beside him. It was too dark to see his face, but his form and his footsteps were unmistakable. Peter had thought he was alone in the barn, but it did not surprise him to know that Benj had been there, too.

"I heard them talking together," Peter whispered excitedly. "Did you hear them, Benj—"

"Aye, I heard them," the old man nodded.

"It was wonderful what they said, wasn't it, Benj?"

"Wonderful, indeed."

Peter took Benj's hand and the two started back to the house across the white barnyard under the star-decked sky.

"It's the same for us as it is for them, isn't it, Benj?"

"Aye, it's the same for us as we all serve the one Father, but only the still of heart can catch that message and link it to their lives."

A few minutes later Peter was ready to close his eyes in

sleep, when he smiled to himself in the darkness of his room. Christmas seemed a more beautiful time than it had ever seemed before—a time when one gave of one's best and rejoiced in the giving because it was one's all.

And then, it was almost as if his mother were standing beside his bed for he could hear her talking to him; but it was not her words, it was the words her mother had used when Martha was a little girl.

"When something wonderful happens to people on Christmas Eve, it is to be cherished in the heart and in the mind. We must not be afraid of the wonderful things, nor must we let others laugh them away from us. Only thus do we learn to hold our dreams—"

Peter smiled to himself again, then he turned his head on his pillow and went to sleep.

Nancy Willard

THE MERRY HISTORY OF
A CHRISTMAS PIE

Devil in a dumpling, ten hands high,
how shall I make my Christmas pie?

Here I come, Sir Cinnamon,
under my hat a thousand men,
and if you don't believe what I say,
here comes Miss Mace to clear the way.

Here I come, Good Mistress Mace,
turning lemons into lace,
and if you don't believe what I say,
here comes Nutmeg to clear the way.

Here I come, clever Nutmeg.
I beat the devil at mumbly peg,
and if you don't believe what I say,
here's Father Salt to clear the way.

Here I come, old Father Salt,
with a jumble of joys and a funnel of faults,
and if you don't believe what I say,
here comes Clove to clear the way.

Here I come, Good Master Clove.
My true love lives behind your stove,
and if you don't believe what I say,
here comes Ginger to clear the way.

Here I come, the Ginger Man.
I comb my hair with a pudding pan,
and if you don't believe what I say,
here comes Pepper to clear the way.

Here I come, saucy Pepper.
I caught a dragon for my supper,
and if you don't believe what I say,
here's Lord Anise to clear the way.

Here I come, Anise the Great.
I burned the pie and ate the plate.

Angel in an eggshell, cricket in a coop,
how shall I make my Christmas soup?

Here I come, Oregano.
I taught a raven how to row,
and if you don't believe what I say,
here's Master Sage to clear the way.

Here I come, wise Master Sage.
I locked my shadow in a cage,
and if you don't believe what I say,
Here's Captain Thyme to clear the way.

Here I come, brave Captain Thyme.
I make my men work overtime,
and if you don't believe what I say,
here comes Coriander to clear the way.

Here I come, old Coriander,
friend of the Emperor Alexander,
and if you don't believe what I say,
here's old man Dill to clear the way.

Here I come, Old Man Dill,
I eat my lunch on the windowsill,
and if you don't believe what I say,
here come the children to clear the way.

Here we come, Miss Rosemary
and Marjoram and Caraway,
and here comes Papa Tarragon,
and now the Christmas soup is done.

Pie in the oven and soup on the fire,
a bowl for the peddler, a bell for the crier,
herbs in the pantry, spices on the shelf,
if you want any more, you must cook it yourself.

Lois Lenski

THE CHRISTMAS FAKE
A Backwoods Christmas

THE RIDLEYS' house stood all alone back in the great piney woods. From the blacktop highway, a shady road wandered in and out around pine trees and palmettos to get to it. Sometimes trucks and wagons got stuck in the loose sand and had to be jacked up before they could be pulled out.

Two old live-oak trees stood near the house, with broken branches and streams of Spanish moss hanging. The unpainted house, built of vertical battens, had turned a dull gray from the ravages of wind and weather. It had a porch across the front and four rooms inside. Under the house, several wild hogs were rooting. Tangled, torn curtains hung at the windows and the front door stood wide open. Blocking the entrance, lay three hound-dogs outstretched. Their names were Trixie, Patches, and Jerry. Daddy insisted they were good watchdogs, but Mom said they were lazy and good for nothing.

Letty was ten, the oldest, Mike seven, and little Punky three. Besides Mom and Dad, there was Mom's sister, Aunt Vi, who spent most of her spare time with them. Mom didn't like living out in the backwoods so far from town, but the owner let them rent the house for almost nothing, so she tried to make the best of it.

The days were still as hot as midsummer. The only way any one could tell that winter was coming was by the shortness of daylight. The sun seemed to set earlier every night. Just as soon as the big red ball slid down into the horizon, the dark dropped down like a heavy black curtain. The short days meant December, and December meant only one thing to the children. Christmas came to them in hot weather, not in cold. Christmas was green to them, never white. Having lived all their lives in the sunny south, they had never seen snow.

"How many days till Christmas?" asked Mike.

Letty, his sister, answered. First it was ten, then only seven, and now it was only one. Christmas was tomorrow.

"I want a doll and a buggy to ride her in," said little Punky.

"I want a bicycle and a BB gun and a football," said Mike.

"Forget it!" said Letty. "You won't get 'em."

"How do you know?" asked Mike.

"I asked Mom," said Letty. "She said there's no money for presents. I asked her if we could have a tree, and she said no money for a tree, either."

"I'll ask Santa Claus," said Mike.

Letty stared at her brother. Mike was seven now. Did he still believe in Santa Claus?

"Mom said she's gonna take us to town to see Santa Claus," Mike went on. "He's coming in a helicopter, landing right in City Park. I'll ask him for what I want."

Letty felt sad. She hated to tell Mike the truth. Let him believe in Santa as long as he could.

"Don't you remember when the man came and took our TV away?" she began. " 'Cause Daddy only made the first payment?"

"Yes, and I fought him," said Mike. "Then he told us we could have it back after . . . Daddy got a job."

"Daddy got a job," said Letty, "but it's way over on the east coast. He can't even get home for Christmas. We never got the TV back either. Don't you know that, Mike?"

"Yes, but we will," said Mike. "Daddy told me so, the last time he was home."

"He's got a job, but still there's no money for anything," said Letty bitterly.

"I know that," said Mike. "So I'll just ask Santa Claus . . ."

It was hopeless, so Letty said no more.

Mom said they could all go to town that afternoon to see Santa Claus. She made them wash their faces and necks and ears and arms and put their feet in the tin tub to get them clean. She got out clean clothes for them and they put shoes and stockings on. Letty's dress was patched, but it held together.

The Ridleys did not have a car. Daddy drove to his new job on the east coast with a neighbor who worked there, too. They left early Monday morning and did not return till late Saturday.

It was only a mile to town, not too far, except when Punky went along and got tired and had to be carried. Today Aunt Vi came by in her Ford and picked Mom and the children up. Aunt Vi had a job in an office in town. She typed letters for a real-estate man. She was having a few days off for Christmas.

When they got to town, Mom went with Aunt Vi to the beauty shop. Aunt Vi was to get a permanent, and Mom had to go to the supermarket for food. The children jumped out at Main Street. "Meet me at the bench at the corner," said Mom, "after Santa Claus leaves." It was too early for Santa Claus now, so Letty took Punky in the dime store. Mike saw some boys and went off with them.

How festive the little town looked! The light posts along the street were trimmed with tinsel and red paper bells. All the stores had Christmas decorations in their windows. From several, loudspeakers were blaring Christmas music. There were many shoppers going in and out. Everybody was happy because Christmas was coming.

Letty started down Main Street, pulling Punky by the hand. Punky broke loose and dashed on ahead. So Letty had to skip along fast to keep up. Inside the store, Punky ran down the aisle and picked things off the counters. Letty made her put them back and slapped her hands.

Letty had two dollars of her own in her pocket. She had earned it baby-sitting for the Boyers. They had four little ones under six and she often sat with them. She went to the jewelry counter. She wanted a pretty brass pin to wear on her shoulder. There were so many it was hard to choose. They were only twenty-five cents. If there wasn't going to be any Christmas at home at least she could buy herself a present. She'd still have $1.75 left to help pay for that new coat she needed.

"Is that your little sister?" asked the clerk.

Letty heard a child crying, but did not look up.

"Yes," she said. "She bothers the daylights out of me. Keeps me runnin' my legs off. I get mad at her. I take her by the arm and jerk her."

"Better watch her now," said the clerk. "She's helping herself to a doll. Guess she's too little to know you have to pay for things in here."

"Do you know what I do to make her mind?" asked Letty.

"No," said the clerk, "but you'd better do it quick."

"I spank her," said Letty. "Not when my mother's around, of course. I spank her with my hand—hard too!"

She rushed over to Punky, took the doll out of her hand, and spanked her. Punky screamed and stamped her foot.

"Now you keep still," said Letty, "or I'll take you home."

Letty dragged her back to the jewelry counter.

"Does spanking make her better?" asked the clerk.

"Well, no," said Letty. "The more I spank her, the more I have to spank her."

Punky ran back to the doll counter. She picked up the doll again.

"She really wants that doll," said the clerk.

"Oh, she wants everything she sees," said Letty. "She's always saying 'gimme, gimme. . . .' "

Punky called out: "I want it, Letty, I want it. . . ."

"Well, you can't have it!" answered Letty. She bent over the jewelry counter again. Should she get the flying bird or the butterfly? The brooches were all so pretty, she could not decide which one she liked best.

"Has she got a doll at home?" asked the clerk.

"No," said Letty. "She's had dozens, but she breaks 'em all up."

"She ought to have one," said the clerk. "Why don't you buy that doll for her? Then maybe you could keep her quiet. A little girl like that needs a doll to love and play with."

Letty looked up startled. What business was it of the clerk's? She opened her purse. In that moment, she had an important decision to make. She looked across to the toy counter, where Punky was holding up the doll. It was just a cheap one. She saw its price tag—49¢. Then she looked down at the butterfly brooch in her hand.

"I'll take this," she said. She handed the clerk a quarter.

The clerk made no comment. She put the brooch in a small paper bag and rang up the money.

Letty rushed over and jerked Punky away from the toy

counter. Punky began to cry. "I want a dolly . . . I want my mama . . . I wanna go home . . ."

The clerk came over and spoke again: "Do you ever read her a story? Or take her for a ride in her little wagon?"

"What wagon?" Letty stared at the clerk. "Punky hasn't got any little wagon."

"She'd be a pretty little girl," said the clerk, "if you'd wash her face."

"She bothers the daylights out of me," said Letty.

Out on the sidewalk, Punky was still crying. Letty leaned over and wiped her tears away.

"Do you want to see Santa Claus?" Letty asked.

"Yes," said Punky.

"We'll go see Santa Claus, and you can ask him for a dolly," said Letty. "Tell him you want a great big doll as big as a baby. . . ."

Punky smiled. "As big as a baby," she said.

The little City Park was crowded now, with children of all sizes and ages. Men from the Jaycees were herding them into a long line.

"Get in line! Take your turn!" the men shouted.

Overhead, a loud buzzing sound could be heard. The children's eyes all turned toward the sky. There, coming closer and closer, was a helicopter. It slowed up, then came straight down in a roped-off open spot. The door opened and Santa Claus stepped out. He was very fat, dressed in a bright red suit, and had a white mustache and a long white beard. The children screamed with delight.

Letty looked over the crowd and finally spotted Mike. She called to him. Mike made his way over to her and they waited their turn, holding Punky tightly by the hands. Once Letty lifted Punky up so she could see Santa Claus.

The children in the line asked for everything under the sun from bicycles, typewriters, and pianos to parakeets, rabbits, and turtles. The line moved slowly toward the big fat Santa Claus.

"We're next!" said Letty, pushing Mike forward.

Mike never forgot for a minute.

"I want a bicycle, a BB gun, and a football," he said in a loud voice.

Santa patted him on the back.

"I'll do what I can for you, Son," he said and shoved him along. "Who's next?"

Now it was Punky's turn. She stared at the big fat man and his white whiskers, half-frightened.

Letty leaned over. "Say what you want, Punky," she prompted. "Tell him you want a buggy and a doll. . . ."

"I want . . ." began Punky. "I want *a great big doll as big as a baby!*"

Santa laughed. "You be a good girl now," he said, "and I'll try to get it for you, Honey."

Then he turned to Letty.

"You're too old . . ." he began.

"I want a watch!" said Letty emphatically. "Not a Mickey Mouse one—I'm too big for that. A real one, I want this time. That's the only thing I want. I don't care if I get candy or anything else—just a wristwatch!"

Santa eyed her coldly.

"What if you don't get it?" he said.

Letty shrugged. "I'll be satisfied with what I get, even if it's nothing. That's all I can do, I reckon."

But Santa was not listening. He had shoved her quickly aside. He was beaming and smiling and making rash promises to all the children coming behind.

When they got out of the crowd, Letty said to Mike, "Oh, I hate that guy!"

"Who?" said Mike.

"That fool of a Santa Claus," said Letty.

Mike's eyes opened wide.

"Why, he's going to bring us . . ." Mike began ". . . the things we asked for!"

"Oh, no, he's not!" cried Letty angrily. "He's tellin' lies—to all the kids in town, makin' them believe he'll bring them anything they ask for!"

Mike's face turned white. "You mean . . . ?"

Punky began to cry.

Letty did not stop there.

"Santa Claus is just a fake—a big Christmas FAKE!" she said. "I don't believe anything like that. Three years ago I knew it. I got up that Christmas-Eve night to see Santa, and it wasn't him. It was Grandma, I saw her—not even Daddy—puttin' presents out."

The sparkle in Mike's eyes faded, as they filled with tears.

Then suddenly Mom and Aunt Vi came up and Aunt Vi told them where the car was parked.

"Did you tell Santa what you want?" asked Aunt Vi.

"Yes," said Punky. "He said he's gonna bring me a dolly."

"I asked for a bike," said Mike, soberly, "but he don't have to bring it if he don't want to."

Letty lagged behind.

She looked around sharply. Mom and Aunt Vi had no packages under their arms and she saw none in Aunt Vi's car. They had gone shopping but had bought nothing. Santa Claus was just a fake, and so was Christmas. Now she was sure of it.

"I'm gonna walk home," she told Mom.

"O.K.," said Mom. "Better get there by suppertime if you want anything to eat."

Letty walked slowly home, with a heavy heart. She hated the decorations on the street now and the sound of the Christmas music. What good was it all? There would be no Christmas at home. Mom had told her so. The only promise Mom made was, if Dad got the day off, they might eat out and go to a show. Whenever they ate out, Letty took two hot dogs and ice cream. What fun was that?

Letty came to a vacant lot, where Christmas trees were being sold. A young man came rushing out and tried to urge her to buy a tree.

What good was a Christmas tree?

Then Letty stopped in her tracks. Maybe . . . maybe they could have a tree, at least. It would be better than no Christmas at all. There was a box of shiny balls and a string of electric lights left over from a couple of years ago. She knew just where they were, on the bottom shelf of the kitchen cupboard.

Why not have a tree . . . with lights on it?

It would be better than nothing. Especially if there

were no presents. Punky would like the pretty lights if she couldn't have a doll-baby.

But the trees were not cheap.

"Two dollars each," said the man, holding one up.

"It's too big," said Letty. "Have you got a smaller one?"

The man found a smaller one, but it was two dollars, too.

Letty looked in her purse. All she had left was $1.75. If only she hadn't bought the brooch.

"You got a car?" asked the man. "Where'll I take it?"

"I'm walking," said Letty. "I'll carry it."

The man laughed as if it was a big joke.

"Carry it?" he cried. "A skinny little kid like you?"

Now he was more friendly.

"I'll tell you what I'll do," he said. He found a nice tree for her.

"This one's a little lopsided, but you can have it for one fifty. That'll leave you twenty-five cents for a taxi. Here's a taxi now."

A man got out of the taxi and Letty got in with her tree. The man called "Merry Christmas" after her. The taxi driver took her and the tree home for twenty-five cents.

It was nearly dark when she got there. Days were short now in December, and night clamped down early. The three dogs were on the porch as usual, Trixie, Patches, and Jerry. They slept on the porch to keep burglars away.

Now they thought Letty was a burglar. They barked and barked as she came up, pulling the tree behind her.

Now everybody would see it. Letty had hoped supper would be over and Punky and Mike in bed and, of course, Dad not home yet. Dad was not coming home for Christmas! She wanted to set the tree up in the front room and surprise them all.

But they were all there eating supper—Aunt Vi, too, of course not Dad. Punky had fallen asleep on the couch. Mom called to Letty but Letty was too excited now to eat supper. She put up the tree all by herself. She found Dad's hammer and fixed a brace at the bottom to keep it from falling over. She found the lights and the cord and put them on. She tied the shiny balls on. She turned the switch and the tree looked beautiful.

Then Punky woke up. How surprised she was to see a tree with lights on it! On Christmas Eve, too!

Punky danced around the tree and tripped over the light cord. She grabbed the cord and pulled it. The lights went out. Punky pulled the colored balls off. She dropped one of them and broke it.

Letty took Punky and spanked her.

She plugged the cord in again and put the balls back on.

At least it was something for Christmas.

Letty was tired now and felt like going to bed. She reached for a hot dog off the table and gulped it down. It was all she wanted to eat. She wasn't hungry.

She and Mike looked at each other. They looked round the house. There were no signs of Christmas—except the tree.

"I paid all my baby-sitting money for it!" Letty bragged.

Mom scolded. "You were saving for a new coat. You need a coat more than we need a tree."

Letty turned to Mike. "Tomorrow's Christmas. No presents anywhere. Didn't I tell you?" she whispered.

It was in the middle of the night when Daddy came and wakened them. That is, it seemed like the middle of the night. It was really six in the morning.

"Merry Christmas! Merry Christmas!" shouted Daddy. When did he come? How did he get there? Did he get an unexpected day off?

Dad was wheeling a bike. Where had it come from?

"But, Mom!" cried Letty. She rubbed her eyes as if she'd been dreaming: "You said there was no money. . . ."

Mike was so happy, he did not ask where the bike came from. He did not notice that it was scuffed and secondhand. It was a bike at last.

Mom was opening a big box beside her. She took a small one out and handed it to Letty. Letty opened it. There lay a wristwatch—a real one, not a Mickey Mouse one. Letty could not believe her eyes.

"So you won't miss the school bus," said Mom.

Letty threw her arms around Mom's neck. Then she hugged Dad.

"You are both FAKES!" she cried. "Mom said there was no money . . . and that Dad couldn't get home. . . ."

Best of all was Punky's doll. It had blue eyes that closed, yellow curls, and white teeth. It was as big as a baby, as big as Punky could hold. She walked up and down, patting the doll and singing to it.

Letty plugged in the lights on the tree. Dad stared. "Where on earth did *that* come from?"

Letty still could not understand. She looked from Mom to Dad. How did they find out about the bike and the watch and the doll? She forgot that she and Mike and Punky had been talking about what they wanted for weeks in advance.

Mike had the answer.

"Santa Claus brought them," he said.

Suddenly Letty thought of something. She ran into the bedroom and came out with a little box. She took out the beautiful butterfly brooch. She had wanted it for herself, but now it was Christmas, so she knew what she wanted to do. She'd give it to Mom.

She turned to Mom and pinned it on her shoulder.

"Merry Christmas, Mom!" she said.

"What! For *me*?" cried Mom.

Mom kissed her and they all said, "Merry Christmas!"

Katherine Paterson

WOODROW KENNINGTON WORKS PRACTICALLY A MIRACLE

"THE FIRST THING I see when I open the door is Sara Jane lying on the rug with my stamp collection all over the place." Woodrow was sitting on the curb in front of his house trying to explain the tragic events of the past hour to his friend Ralph. "My *stamp* collection!"

Ralph was doing his best to sound sympathetic. "Geez," he said.

"I start screaming like an idiot, 'What the hell you think you're doing?' She says—you know how she sticks up her eyebrow—only five-year-old I ever heard of could poke up one eyebrow—she says, cool as can be, 'Hi, Whoodrow.' Blowing my name out like birthday candles. 'Hi, Whoodrow. I'm playing post office.' *Post office!*" Woodrow bent over in pain. "Post office with practically priceless stamps I inherited from my grandfather. I was practically crying out loud. 'Why? Why?' " Woodrow spread out both arms, imitating himself. " 'Why are you playing post office with my stamps?' "

"And she says?"

"She says—get this—she says, 'Don't be stoopid, Whoodrow. You gotta have stamps to play post office.' "

"Oh, yeah?" Ralph grinned and poked him in the ribs with an elbow. "Just ask Jennifer Leonard."

"Shut up, Ralph. You haven't even heard the worst part yet."

Ralph tried to get properly serious. "There's a worst part?"

"About this time my mother comes rushing in, in a bathrobe. It is three thirty in the afternoon. My sister has destroyed an entire fortune in rare stamps while my mother has been taking a nap."

"Yeah?"

"The *reason* she has been taking a nap and let my juvenile-delinquent sister run wild—she takes me off to the den and shuts the door to tell me this goody—the reason she laid down and took her eye off Sara Jane 'for one minute' is that she is pregnant."

"Yeah?"

"My mother is thirty-eight years old."

"So?"

"Ralph, she is too old already to handle Sara Jane."

. . .

At about eight that evening Ralph called. After the usual questions about homework had been taken care of, he said, "You know I been thinking about what you told me. I don't think you should be too upset."

"Ralph! That was a practically priceless stamp collection!"

"No, I don't mean about the stamps. I mean about becoming a brother again. Wood, face it. You got no place to go but up, man. When this next kid is five, you're sixteen. Sixteen. You know what a sixteen-year-old guy looks like to a five-year-old? Geez. This kid is liable to worship you."

It was not the worst idea Ralph had ever had. In fact, the more Woodrow thought about it, the better it sounded. His mother was surprised and delighted when he started going out of his way to help her. She began to treat him more and more like an adult. She even asked him to try to get Sara Jane to accept the idea of a new baby.

This was no small problem. Sara Jane had expressed neither excitement nor resentment when they told her. She simply pretended that she hadn't heard. Once when he was baby-sitting, Woodrow tried very hard to explain the whole situation to her. He even threw in a few interesting facts of life as a bonus.

"Don't be stoopid, Whoodrow." She never mentioned the subject again, or even seemed to hear others mention it, until the day she found Woodrow and his mother putting together the old baby bed in her room.

She marched in, hands on hips. "Get this junk outta my room."

"Sara Jane, it's for the baby." Mother was super patient. "You remember, I talked to you yesterday. . . ."

"I'm not having no baby."

"We're all having a baby, Sara Jane."

"Not me."

"OK. *I'm* having a baby, but . . ."

"Then put this junk in your own room."

"But darling, I explained, there's no place. . . ."

Woodrow offered on the spot to take the baby into his room. His mother stalled and his father fumed, but eventually the bed, bureau, and rocking chair took the place of his racing car setup. His father bought a screen and covered it with airline posters, but he needn't have. Woodrow was not feeling anything like a martyr. It was the chance of a lifetime. He would start this kid out right. No more Sara Janes for him.

As for Sara Jane, she would come to Woodrow's door and stand there with her hands on her hips, her eyebrow elevated, staring at the crib legs peeking out below the bottom of the screen, but she never said a word. Occasionally, though, she would sigh—a sigh as long and weary as the *whooo-oosh* of his mother's ancient percolator. It made Woodrow uneasy, but not prepared for what happened next. He wondered later if he should have been prepared. Shouldn't he have taken a cue from her strange shift in TV programs? What normal kid would move in the span of two weeks from *Electric Company* to *Speed Racer* to, of all things, *The One True Word*, starring Brother Austin Barnes? He had really meant to ask her about it, but the switch took place in the last wild days before the baby was born, and frankly, everyone was so glad to have her quiet and occupied that they neglected to keep a proper check on what she was watching.

When his father called from the hospital at seven o'clock to tell him that he had a brother, Woodrow let out a whoop that could have been heard for blocks. It brought Sara Jane out of the den into the kitchen. "It's a boy!" Woodrow yelled at her. "A boy!"

She watched him with a very peculiar expression on her face—neither anger nor surprise, certainly not delight. Where had he seen it before? A memory of old fading pictures in the back of the Sunday School closet came to his mind—it was that same sickly sweet half smile.

Then she let him have it. "Brother Whoodrow," she said. "I saw Jesus today."

"You what?"

Her smile, if anything, got more sickly. "I said, 'I saw Jesus.'"

Surely it was that religious program she had been watching—that combined with the shock of the news he had just given her. He felt very generous, almost sorry for her, so he tried to be kindly. "So you saw Jesus, huh?"

"I was walking home from school. All alone. Nobody meets me halfway anymore. Mommy got too fat, and Mrs. Judson is too lazy." She paused to let these sad words sink in. "But Jesus loves me. Just like Brother Austin says. When Jesus saw me coming home from school, he stopped his big black car. 'Hi,' he says."

"Sara Jane, that wasn't Jesus. He never had any big black car."

"He does now."

Woodrow was beginning to feel panicky. "Did he ask you to get into the car or anything?"

"No," she said primly.

He was not about to let Sara Jane get kidnapped while his mother was in the hospital. He told Mrs. Judson, who was staying there days, that Sara Jane had to be met at the school door. Mrs. Judson read one of those newspapers that never hesitate to give all the gory details, so when he told her about the big black car, she made the trip to the kindergarten door every day, lazy or not.

In the meantime, Daniel came home. He was the greatest baby in the world, even when he cried. In fact, Woodrow's favorite time was when Daniel cried at two o'clock in the morning. His mother would fuss and apologize when she'd come in and find Woodrow awake, but then they'd talk while she fed the baby. What a warm, good feeling to be talking in the middle of the night—grown-up to grown-up. It would have been the happiest time of his life except for Sara Jane.

He may have saved her from kidnapping, but he certainly hadn't solved the real problem. He wasn't sure if he was going to be able to stand it. Sara Jane the screaming baby, he had endured. Sara Jane the unbearable brat, he had gotten more or less used to. But Sara Jane the Saint was about to do him in.

Ralph thought it was the funniest thing since Whoopee cushions, but he didn't have to live with her. She was always smiling at him and calling him Brother Whoodrow and begging him to watch *The One True Word* with her.

She prayed all the time. If Mrs. Judson fussed at her, she would go into her room and fall on her knees, praying that God would forgive poor bad Mrs. Judson. It was Woodrow's job to fix breakfast for the two of them. Sara Jane would bless the food until the toast had turned to floor tile.

But even that he might have put up with had she not announced to him one morning that their parents were going to Hell.

"Shut up, Sara Jane."

"But they're lost!" she said.

"They are not lost. They're Presbyterians."

"See? They don't even know they're lost and going to Hell."

"Well, why don't you just tell them?"

"They'd laugh at me."

They would, too. He wanted to laugh himself, but he couldn't quite. Suppose his father and mother were headed for Hell and didn't even know it? Suppose he were? They were all bound for Hell while Sara Jane . . . Suddenly, as the robots would say, it did not compute. Sara Jane the Saint was pure plastic—the fake of all fakes. Instead of letting her scare him, he should be whipping her back into shape. It was up to him to get her back to normal. Normal, mind you, was never all that great, but normal he could manage.

First, he would silence *The One True Word.* Fortunately, the TV set was practically an antique, which meant all he had to do was take a couple of tubes out of the back and hide them in his bureau drawer beneath his underwear.

When Sara Jane complained to her father that the TV was broken, he hardly looked up from his newspaper. He didn't like TV anyhow, which was why he'd never bothered to get a decent set, much less color.

"Who is going to fix the TV?" she persisted.

Her father put down his paper. "Nobody has time to bother with that TV before Christmas. Besides"—he was already back behind the paper—"you watch too much TV anyway."

Woodrow found her some minutes later on her knees in the den, her hand on the cold set. "O Lord"—Woodrow wasn't sure if she were praying aloud for his benefit or God's—"O Lord, make this TV set well. The Devil broke it, but you can make it well."

"Sara Jane!" He was so shocked that he burst right into her prayer. She ignored him and kept on rocking and praying. Woodrow was not crazy about being called the Devil, but he sure as heck was not going to put the tubes back now and turn the kid into a permanent religious weirdo.

Next morning at breakfast, there were no lengthy announcements. Sara Jane just rolled her eyes up at the ceiling and said, "OK, God. You know what you gotta do." And in answer to Woodrow's openmouthed stare, she said, "He knows if he doesn't hurry up and fix that set, I'm not going to believe in him anymore."

When he came in from school two days in a row to find her praying over the TV set, he began to weaken. "How about me taking you Christmas shopping, Sara Jane?"

Slowly she turned and gave him her saddest face. "I guess I'm not going to believe in Christmas this year. The TV still doesn't work."

"Oh"—his voice sounded very cheery and very fakey —"I wouldn't give up on Christmas just because of some old TV. Maybe it's just a broken tube or something."

"God can do anything he wants to. If he doesn't want to fix this TV, it means he doesn't want me to be his child. I guess nobody wants me to be their child."

Ralph, after he stopped laughing, suggested that Woodrow launch a campaign. It was obvious that the child felt insecure. Woodrow needed to prove to her that her family really loved her. Then she would be cured.

Woodrow was desperate enough to try anything, even a suggestion from Ralph. He persuaded his mother that she was not too tired to make cookies with Sara Jane, since he, Woodrow, would clean up the entire kitchen afterward. Sara Jane made twelve gorgeous gingerbread men, all scowling. Woodrow talked his father into taking Sara Jane on a special trip to see Santa Claus. She had climbed, after much urging, onto the old fellow's lap, only to ask him why his breath smelled all mediciny. Woodrow himself devoted a full Saturday morning to helping Sara Jane make a crèche out of baker's dough.

"Sara Jane." He tried not to sound too critical. "We can't use fourteen snakes in one manger scene."

"That's all I feel like making, Whoodrow. Just snakes and snakes"—she sighed—"Dead snakes."

"Suppose," he said, his eyes carefully on the sheep he

was modeling, "suppose the TV would get well. Would you feel better then?"

"It's too late. God flunked already."

"Maybe he just needed a little more time, or something."

She looked him dead in the eye. "If the TV got fixed now, I'd know it was you or daddy did it. Just to shut me up. You're just scared I'm going to mess up your old Christmas. That's all you care about."

He tried to protest, but she was too close to the truth. How could he enjoy Christmas when he felt like some kind of a monster?

Christmas Eve their parents went off to church, leaving him in charge. There had been a bit of trouble earlier when Sara Jane had refused at first to hang up her stocking. "I just don't believe in Christmas anymore," she had said wearily. Their parents hadn't known whether to take her seriously or not, but Woodrow had. He whispered in her ear that if she didn't hang up her stocking that minute he was going to beat the you-know-what out of her the minute the folks walked out the door. She sighed, that long now-frequent sigh of hers, and handed him her stocking to put up.

After he had gotten her, still moaning and sighing, into bed, he sank into the big living-room chair, staring miserably at the blinking lights of the Christmas tree. The tree itself looked so fat and jolly and merry that he was close to tears when the telephone rang.

It was Ralph. He was baby-sitting, too, but he was so cheerful it made Woodrow feel murderous. "Say, there's this great movie on Channel Seven. It was practically X-rated when it first came out."

"Our TV's broken, remember?"

Ralph chortled. "I also remember, old buddy, that you can work that little miracle whenever you want to."

Woodrow slammed down the receiver. Everything always seemed simple to Ralph. When Ralph looked at his Christmas tree, he didn't have to see at its base fourteen dead snakes guarding a manger scene. If only he could fix everything as easily as he could fix that blasted TV. Well, what the heck? A practically X-rated movie was sure to take his mind off Sara Jane for a little while.

He dug the tubes out of his underwear drawer and put them back into the TV set. The old set warmed as slowly as ever, gradually filling the den with the sound of Christmas music. He reached out to switch the channel, but before he could do so, the hundred-voiced TV choir sang a line that made his fingers stop in midair.

"See him in a manger laid whom the angels praise above. . . ."

I saw Jesus today. That's what Sara Jane had said that had started this whole mess. What was so wrong, after all, with a lonesome little kid, even a bad—maybe especially a bad—little lonesome kid wanting some proof that God cared about her? It was not as if she were eleven and needed to face the facts. Maybe Ralph had an idea, after all. Maybe Woodrow could work a little miracle.

He took the hedge clipper out to the backyard and cut so much dried grass and weeds that it took him four or five trips to carry it all in. He dumped his underwear on the bed, put his pillow into the drawer, and covered it with grass. The rest of the grass and weeds he scattered across the living-room floor. He put the drawer on a footstool in front of the Christmas tree. The knobs were showing, so he turned it around. He turned off the blinking lights. The lighting had to be just so, or it wouldn't work. He tried a single candle on the end table. Better. He experimented with the music from the TV in the den until he got it just loud enough to sound sort of mysterious. Then, very carefully, his heart thumping madly against his chest, he lifted the still-sleeping Daniel from his bed, wrapped him in a crib sheet, and laid him in the drawer. When he was satisfied that everything was perfect, he wrapped his own top sheet around himself and went to get Sara Jane.

He shook her and then stepped back near the door. "Sara Jane!" He made his voice strong and slightly spooky. "Sara Jane!" She stirred in her sleep. "Sara Jane Kennington!"

Slowly Sara Jane sat up.

"Sara Jane!" She was looking around trying to figure out, perhaps, where the voice was coming from, so he hiked up his sheet and spread his arms out wide. "Arise!" he commanded. "Arise and follow me!"

Now she saw him—at least she turned and looked straight at him—but when she slid out of bed and padded toward the door, it was as though she were sleepwalking. He turned quickly and led her down the hall. Just as they got to the doorway into the living room, he stepped back and gestured for her to go ahead.

She went on for a few steps and then stopped. He

watched her back. Her thin little body was shivering under her pajamas. Her head moved back and forth very slowly. She was taking the whole scene in. And it was beautiful. Even when you knew. Like that painting of the shepherds in the dark barn where the only light comes from the manger. The baby had worked his arms and legs loose from the sheet and was waving them in the air. Above the angel music you could hear his happy bubbling noises.

"Ohh." Sara Jane let out such a long sigh that her whole body shuddered. "Ohhh." She dared a tiny step forward. "Hi, Jesus," she said.

There was something so quiet, so pure, about the way she said it that it went straight through to Woodrow's stomach. He found he was shaking all over. Why was he so cold and scared? He had fooled her, hadn't he? He ought to be feeling proud, not sick to his stomach.

Sara Jane took another step toward the baby. Now what was he supposed to do? He hadn't given any thought to what he should do *after* the miracle. Stupid. Stupid. Stupid. He reached out to stop her from going any farther and stumbled over his sheet. "Oh, hell!"

She turned around, half afraid, half puzzled. "Whoodrow?"

"Don't be scared, Sara Jane. It's just me." He disentangled himself from the sheet. "Stoopid old Whoodrow." The choir from the den launched into a series of hallelujahs. "Oh, shut up!"

Sara Jane in the candlelight might have been a little princess waking from an enchanted sleep. Finally, she cocked her head. "Is that the TV?" she asked.

"Yeah." He turned on the 150-watt reading lamp. "I fixed it."

She blinked a moment in the brightness, and then marched over to the fake manger. "That's Daniel in there."

"Yeah." He was beginning to feel hot. "I was trying to fool you." He flopped heavily to the couch. "Sara Jane, for your future information, nobody should go around trying to fake miracles. First, I broke the TV so you wouldn't be religious, and then I fixed all this junk"—he waved his arm around the room—"so you would. Go ahead. Say it. I'm stoopid."

She came over to the couch and ducked her head so she could look up into his face. "This wasn't stoopid," she said. "I liked it."

She must not understand what he was trying to say. He repeated himself. "I was the one that broke the TV set in the first place."

"Huh?"

"I couldn't stand you praying and acting good all the time."

She looked surprised. "I thought you wanted me to be good, Whoodrow. You used to hate me when I was bad."

"I never hated you. Honest."

"Well"—she sighed her old weary sigh—"Mommy and Daddy did. They wouldn't have got a new one if they liked the old one."

His shame began to shift in the direction of the old exasperation. "Sara Jane Kennington, do you think they stopped liking me when you were born? Maybe they loved me even better than before."

"Really?" He thought she was going to smile, but instead her face clouded up. "Well, I know for sure God hates me. I been so bad." Her chin began to quiver. "I know for sure God hates me."

"Sara Jane. God is crazy about you."

First her eyebrow went up; then she giggled. "You're stoopid, Whoodrow."

"Maybe so," he said. "And then again, maybe not."

When he thought about it later, Woodrow wondered if his miracle had been so fake after all. Ralph's definition of a miracle was something that no one in his right mind would believe. And Ralph, for one, could not believe that Woodrow Kennington had spent Christmas Eve raking grass off his living-room floor while listening happily to his sister sing through practically the entire "Hallelujah Chorus" accompanied by a silver-voiced choir of thousands. In fact, now that Sara Jane was back to normal, he had some trouble believing it himself.

Rachel Field

ALL THROUGH THE NIGHT

ALL THAT DAY the Inn yard had been thronged with people coming to pay their taxes in the town of Bethlehem. The small sturdy watchdog who slept in the stable and picked up what food he could find had never before seen such a crowd of travelers.

When night fell he was tired from barking at so many strangers and their beasts, and with scurrying out of the way of feet and hoofs. But for all the barking and running about it had been a good day. The Inn had overflowed into the yard. There had been a fire there with meat roasting over it and pots that sent out clouds of savory steam. Many a rich morsel had fallen his way, so he felt well content as he crept into his corner of the stable near the oxen's stall.

He and they greeted each other and exchanged news of the day.

"Yes, we, too, have been busy," the oxen told him. "Heavy loads for us since daybreak and the roads round Bethlehem so choked with carts and caravans and herds and flocks we could hardly move sometimes."

"And rude, stupid creatures they were to meet!" the ass put in from her corner. "With no manners at all or sense enough to follow their own noses. Some even dared to dispute the right of way with me, but I held my ground."

"I have no doubt you did," said the dog, for he knew the ass was not one to be persuaded against her will. He turned himself round and round in a pile of straw to make himself comfortable and fell to licking a bruised spot on his leg.

"There must have been many sheep," the old ewe joined in from her pen. "I could not see them because I was shut in here with my two lambs, but I could tell by their voices that some came from places farther away than Judea. I should have liked to see them."

"Well," the dog told her, "I found them a dusty, frightened lot. I was thankful not to have their herding in my charge. And the goats were no better," he added, that the bearded gray goat might be sure to hear. He and the goat were not upon friendly terms and took pleasure in tormenting each other.

"Peace and quiet. Peace and quiet at last," the doves cooed from the rafters. "Peace and quiet till morning, that is all we ask."

The hens made soft clucking sounds to show that they were in complete agreement.

But the cock with his scarlet comb and burnished tail feathers, stepping about in search of stray kernels, was of a different mind. "I like noise and bustle myself." He voiced his opinion loudly. "Peace is all very well for those who haven't the spirit for something better. Now *I* can hardly wait for morning."

"Everyone to his own taste," the mild-eyed cow put in her word, shifting her cud deftly and flicking her tail as she did so. "If it were always day or always night we should not all be satisfied."

"Well said. Well said," the doves agreed in drowsy unison from the dimness of the eaves.

Darkness gathered there first. The swallows were already seeking their nests, while the bats were beginning to stretch and unfold their lean, black wings.

Night was coming fast and all the birds and beasts and insects of the stable knew that it belonged to them. The world was theirs as the world of day could never be. When the sun rose man would be their master again. They would carry his burdens or feed or serve him according to their different gifts. But night was their own, when they might move or fight or take counsel together without man's interference. It was good that this should be so, the little dog thought, as he burrowed deeper into the straw.

His sworn enemy the cat slid by. She moved like a shadow with fiery-green eyes ready to pounce upon the mice who were already squeaking and scampering at their play. But the dog was too tired and comfortable to give chase, so for once he let her pass unmolested. All about him crickets chirped in rusty chorus and sometimes a bat swooped so low he could feel the stir of its wings. The darkness was warm and alive with the familiar scents of fur and feathers and grain and straw.

"Rest well. Rest well. Rest well." The doves cooed sleepily, making a soft sound in their throats that was like the bubbling of a well-filled pot over a fire.

Night had come to Bethlehem. The Inn had been full hours ago. The dog could hear late travelers being turned away. The stable door was securely bolted against intruders and the wind was rising, frosty and keen. Through an opening in the roof a star shone bright as purest silver.

"I never saw a star look so large or so near," the cock observed as he moved about with his spurred, high-stepping walk. "Somehow it makes me very restless, and there is something strange in the air. Perhaps you have felt it, too?"

But the dog made no answer. He yawned and laid his pointed muzzle on his paws and prepared himself for sleep.

He woke at the sound of voices outside and roused himself to bark. But though the hair rose along his back, no sound came rumbling from his throat. The bolt was drawn and the stable door opened to lantern light and the dim shapes of two men and a donkey on whose back a woman sat, wrapped in a heavy cloak.

"Well"—the voice of the Inn Keeper sounded short and impatient—"if you cannot go on, there is only the stable to offer. Coming as you have at such an hour, you are fortunate to have this shelter till morning."

"The roads were crowded," the Man answered him, "and our pace was slow because of my wife. You can see that she is nearly spent."

"Yes, yes." The Inn Keeper was already shutting the door. "I am sorry for your plight, but I tell you there is no room left."

The dog was on his feet. He could hear the other animals rising about him, yet not one of them uttered a sound. Their throats were as silent as his own.

In the flickering lantern light he watched the Man lift the Woman from the donkey's back and set her upon her feet. She was so weary she would have fallen but for the Man's arms.

"Joseph," she said, "you must not be troubled for me, even if it should be that the time has come. . . ." She rested her head on the Man's shoulder and sighed so softly it might have been one of the doves in the rafters drawing closer to her mate.

"But, Mary," the Man went on, "it is not right and fitting that it should be here—not in a stable among the beasts."

"Who knows," she comforted him, "what is to be? These beasts are more kind than men who kill and hurt one another. I am glad to be here. Their warm breath comforts me. Their straw is clean and soft to rest upon."

Everywhere beyond the ring of light that the lantern made, bright eyes were upon the strangers. Furry ears and quivering noses pointed, alert and watchful.

The strange donkey, freed of his load, found a place

beside the ass. He sank down, too tired to drink water from the trough or reach for a mouthful of hay.

A hush was on the stable. Not only were all throats silent, but no wings stirred; no claws scratched and not a hoof pounded. And in that hour nothing died. The young swallows and mice were safe from their enemies, for a mystery greater than death held them all in its power.

The lantern flickered and went out.

"Our oil is gone!" the Man cried out in distress.

"There will be light enough." The Woman spoke in a faint voice, and as if in answer the star in the roof gap shone brighter than before.

How long it was after that the little dog could not tell. Morning was still far off, yet the cock suddenly lifted up his voice, so shrill and clear it seemed he would split himself in two. It was not like any other cockcrow since the world began and it rose higher than the rafters and mounted to heaven itself. At the same instant each creature found voice and joined with him. Every living thing in the stable had a part in that swelling chorus of praise. Even the bees hummed till their hive throbbed with music, sweeter than all its store of honey.

"What manner of place is this?" the Man cried out. "What beasts are these who have the tongues of angels?"

But the Woman answered him softly out of the shadows. "It was they who gave us shelter this night. Let them draw near and be the first to worship."

She drew aside the folds of her cloak and light filled the stable even to the farthest corners. The dog cowered before such strange brightness. When he dared to look more closely he saw that it encircled the head of an infant, new born.

"There is no bed for him to lie upon," the Man sighed. "Only this"—and he pointed to the manger.

"Bring it here," the Mother said. "My heart tells me there will be nights when he will have no place at all to rest his head."

So the Child lay quiet in the straw-filled wooden manger and all the animals came to view him there—the oxen, the cow, the ass and the donkey, the ewe and her lambs, the gray goat, the dog, the hens and the proud cock ruffling his feathers. The cat left off her prowling to join them and the mice ran beside her without fear. The crickets came, too, drawn from the comfort of their warm straw; the bees, from their snug hive. The tireless ants and spiders left their toil to draw near. The swallows in the eaves flew down; the bats bent low on their dark wings, and the doves came closest of all with their soft murmurs above the manger. When they had all seen the Wonder they returned to their places and were quiet again.

All but the dog. He could not rest as he had before. He stretched himself beside the manger and lay with his head on his folded paws, his eyes wide and watchful as the hours passed.

Long before sunrise the door opened without sound of bolt being drawn and a band of Shepherds came in. They bore a strange tale on their lips and they also worshiped on bended knees. One carried a lamb in his arms and the Child answered its bleating with a smile.

"Behold the Lamb of God," they said one to another
as they turned to go back to their flocks on the hills.

The star grew pale and through the gap in the stable
roof morning showed rosy in the east. Even before the cock
hailed it, the dog knew that the sun was up. But he did not
move lest he rouse the three in his care. It was then that he
saw a strange thing.

The rafters high above cast their shadows as the rising
sun struck through. Two of the beams crossed in sharp
black bars that fell directly across the sleeping Child. The
little dog could not tell why the sight should make him
cower in sudden fear.

Then the cock crowed three times and the first sounds
of people stirring in the Inn and yard began.

He watched the Man and the Woman preparing to go.
He saw the donkey being watered and fed and the blanket
fitted in place. He saw the Mother wrap her Son warmly
against the cold before the Man set them upon the donkey's back and lifted a heavy bundle on his own.

"Come," he said and opened the stable door. "We
must make haste."

Stiff from his long vigil, the dog rose and followed
them to the door. He watched them cross the Inn yard in
the early light and join other travelers who were already
thronging the roads leading to and from Bethlehem. Soon
they would be lost to his sight, those Three whom he had
guarded through the hours of darkness.

"Ah," cried the cock, preening his burnished feathers,
"what a morning!" He strutted over to where bits of food

and grain lay scattered and began to forage for stray morsels.

The dog lifted his head and sniffed hungrily. He could tell that pots were already on the fires. The sharp morning air brought the savory news to him and he knew that by keeping close to the kitchen he would soon be well filled. He remembered a bone he had buried yesterday in a secluded spot. Yet he did not seek it. He trotted past the kitchen doors, and though his nose twitched at the smells that he was leaving he kept it pointed straight ahead.

"Wait. Wait." His bark rang out sharp and determined and his paws clicked over the stones as he ran.

He did not pause till he had caught up with the Man who led the plodding donkey and his burden along the dusty road.

"Here I am!" He barked again as he fell into step beside them. "Let me come with you."

Ruth Sawyer

THE CHRISTMAS APPLE

ONCE UPON A TIME there lived in Germany a little clockmaker by the name of Hermann Joseph. He lived in one little room with a bench for his work, and a chest for his wood, and his tools, and a cupboard for dishes, and a trundle bed under the bench. Besides these there was a stool, and that was all—excepting the clocks.

There were hundreds of clocks: little and big, carved and plain, some with wooden faces and some with porcelain ones—shelf clocks, cuckoo clocks, clocks with chimes and clocks without; and they all hung on the walls, covering them quite up.

In front of his one little window there was a little shelf,

and on this Hermann put all his best clocks to show the passersby. Often they would stop and look, and someone would cry: "See, Hermann Joseph has made a new clock. It is finer than any of the rest!"

Then if it happened that anybody was wanting a clock, he would come in and buy it.

I said Hermann was a little clockmaker. That was because his back was bent and his legs were crooked, which made him very short and funny to look at. But there was no kinder face than his in all the city, and the children loved him. Whenever a toy was broken or a doll had lost an arm or a leg or an eye, its careless *Mütterchen* would carry it straight to Hermann's little shop.

"The *Kindlein* needs mending," she would say. "Canst thou do it now for me?"

And whatever work Hermann was doing he would always put aside to mend the broken toy or doll, and never a pfennig would he take for the mending.

"Go spend it for sweetmeats or, better still, put it by till Christmas time. 'Twill get thee some happiness then, maybe," he would always say.

Now it was the custom in that long-ago for those who lived in the city to bring gifts to the great cathedral on Christmas and lay them before the Holy Mother and Child. People saved all through the year that they might have something wonderful to bring on that day; and there was a saying among them that, when a gift was brought that pleased the Christ Child more than any other, He would reach down from Mary's arms and take it.

This was but a saying, of course. The old Herr Graff,

the oldest man in the city, could not remember that it had ever really happened; and many there were who laughed at the very idea. But children often talked about it, and the poets made beautiful verses about it; and often when a rich gift was placed beside the altar the watchers would whisper among themselves: "Perhaps now we shall see the miracle."

Those who had no gifts to bring went to the cathedral just the same on Christmas Eve to see the gifts of the others and hear the carols and watch the burning of the waxen tapers. The little clockmaker was one of these. Often he was stopped and someone would ask, "How happens it that you never bring a gift?" Once the Bishop himself questioned him: "Poorer than thou have brought offerings to the Child. Where is thy gift?"

Then it was that Hermann had answered: "Wait; someday you shall see. I, too, shall bring a gift someday."

The truth of it was that the little clockmaker was so busy giving away all the year that there was never anything left at Christmas time. But he had a wonderful idea on which he was working every minute that he could spare time from his clocks. It had taken him years and years; no one knew anything about it but Trude, his neighbor's child, and Trude had grown from a baby into a little housemother and still the gift was not finished.

It was to be a clock, the most wonderful and beautiful clock ever made; and every part of it had been fashioned with loving care. The case, the works, the weights, the hands, and the face, all had taken years of labor. He had spent years carving the case and hands, years perfecting the works; and now Hermann saw that with a little more haste and time he could finish it for the coming Christmas.

He mended the children's toys as before, but he gave up making his regular clocks, so there were fewer to sell, and often his cupboard was empty and he went supperless to bed. But that only made him a little thinner and his face a little kinder; and meantime the gift clock became more and more beautiful.

It was fashioned after a rude stable with rafters, stall, and crib. The Holy Mother knelt beside the manger in which a tiny Christ Child lay, while through the open door the hours came. Three were kings and three were shepherds and three were soldiers and three were angels; and when the hours struck, the figure knelt in adoration before the sleeping Child, while the silver chimes played the "Magnificat."

"Thou seest," said the clockmaker to Trude, "it is not just on Sundays and holidays that we should remember to worship the *Krist Kindlein* and bring Him gifts—but every day, every hour."

The days went by like clouds scudding before a winter wind and the clock was finished at last. So happy was Hermann with his work that he put the gift clock on the shelf before the little window to show the passersby. There were crowds looking at it all day long, and many would whisper: "Do you think this can be the gift Hermann has spoken of —his offering on Christmas Eve to the Church?"

The day before Christmas came. Hermann cleaned up his little shop, wound all his clocks, brushed his clothes, and then went over the gift clock again to be sure everything was perfect.

"It will not look meanly beside the other gifts," he thought happily. In fact he was so happy that he gave away all but one pfennig to the blind beggar who passed his door; and then, remembering that he had eaten nothing since breakfast, he spent that last pfennig for a Christmas apple to eat with a crust of bread he had. These he was putting by in the cupboard to eat after he was dressed, when the door opened and Trude was standing there crying softly.

"*Kindlein—Kindlein,* what ails thee?" And he gathered her into his arms.

" 'Tis the father. He is hurt, and all the money that was put by for the tree and sweets and toys has gone to Herr Doktor. And now, how can I tell the children? Already they have lighted the candle at the window and are waiting for Kriss Kringle to come."

The clockmaker laughed merrily.

"Come, come, little one, all will be well. Hermann will sell a clock for thee. Some house in the city must need a clock; and in a wink we shall have money enough for the tree and the toys. Go home and sing."

He buttoned on his greatcoat and, picking out the best of the old clocks, he went out. He went first to the rich merchants, but their houses were full of clocks; then to the journeymen, but they said his clock was old-fashioned. He even stood on the corner of the streets and in the square, crying, "A clock—a good clock for sale," but no one paid any attention to him. At last he gathered up his courage and went to the Herr Graff himself.

"Will your Excellency buy a clock?" he said, trembling at his own boldness. "I would not ask, but it is Christmas and I am needing to buy happiness for some children."

The Herr Graff smiled.

"Yes, I will buy a clock, but not that one. I will pay a thousand gulden for the clock thou hast had in thy window these four days past."

"But, your Excellency, that is impossible!" And poor Hermann trembled harder than ever.

"Poof! Nothing is impossible. That clock or none. Get thee home and I will send for it in half an hour and pay thee the gulden."

The little clockmaker stumbled out.

"Anything but that—anything but that!" he kept mumbling over and over to himself on his way home. But as he passed the neighbor's house he saw the children at the window with their lighted candle, and he heard Trude singing.

And so it happened that the servant who came from the Herr Graff carried the gift clock away with him; but the clockmaker would take but five of the thousand gulden in payment. And as the servant disappeared up the street the chimes commenced to ring from the great cathedral, and the streets suddenly became noisy with the many people going thither bearing their Christmas offerings.

"I have gone empty-handed before," said the little clockmaker sadly. "I can go empty-handed once again." And again he buttoned up his greatcoat.

As he turned to shut his cupboard door behind him his eyes fell on the Christmas apple, and an odd little smile crept into the corners of his mouth and lighted his eyes.

"It is all I have—my dinner for two days. I will carry that to the Christ Child. It is better, after all, than going empty-handed."

How full of peace and beauty was the great cathedral when Hermann entered it! There were a thousand tapers burning, and everywhere the sweet scent of the Christmas greens—and the laden altar before the Holy Mother and Child.

There were richer gifts than had been brought for many years: marvelously wrought vessels from the greatest silversmiths; cloth of gold and cloth of silk brought from the East by the merchants; poets had brought their songs illuminated on rolls of heavy parchment; painters had brought their pictures of saints and the Holy Family; even the King himself had brought his crown and scepter to lay before the Child. And after all these offerings came the little clockmaker, walking slowly down the long, dim aisle holding tight to his Christmas apple.

The people saw him and a murmur rose, hummed a moment indistinctly through the church, and then grew clear and articulate: "Shame! See, he is too mean to bring his clock! He hoards it as a miser hoards his gold. See what he brings! Shame!"

The words reached Hermann and he stumbled on blindly; his head dropped forward on his breast, his hands groping the way. The distance seemed interminable. Now he knew he was past the seats; now his feet touched the first step, and there were seven to climb to the altar. Would his feet never reach the top?

"One, two, three," he counted to himself, then tripped and almost fell. "Four, five, six." He was nearly there. There was but one more.

The murmur of shame died away and in its place rose one of wonder and awe. Soon the words became intelligible: "The miracle! It is the miracle!"

The people knelt in the big cathedral; the Bishop raised his hands in prayer. And the little clockmaker, stumbling to the last step, looked up through dim eyes and saw the Child leaning toward him, far down from Mary's arms, with hands outstretched to take his gift.

Ruth Sawyer

A CANDLE FOR
ST. BRIDGET

An Irish Tale of an
American Christmas

FTER A DECADE the words of old Michael Donnelly come back to me again: "Aye, it takes more nor a handful o' years for a good tale to ripen."

And why not? Old wine, old friends, need the test of time to prove their excellence; why should we hasten the mellowing of a good story? Here, at any rate, is one that is well ripened. It has to do with Michael Donnelly himself, and with his kindred. It would have slipped entirely from my memory if I had not chanced into the Little Church of St. Anthony the other day and found a single candle burning before a saint.

Long ago I went into Ireland, presumably to interview

Sir Horace Plunkett about the Congested District Board and his dairy and cottage industries; what I actually did was to follow the trail of Irish folk and fairy lore and search out every likely story-teller from Mallin Head to Cork. That is how I came upon Michael Donnelly in his little cabin on the moors of Donegal.

The cabin was perched alone at the very borderland where moorland stopped and the rough, sea-hewn cliffs of the Ulster coast began. There was another cabin, I remember, in the hollow of the land a mile or so back; but for that, east, west, north, and south there wasn't another sign of life except the sea-mews that whirled and screamed over the cliffs where they had made their nests and the lean brown hares that had burrowed in the sand dunes and hunted the moors for their scanty food.

Michael Donnelly was among the last of the old Skanachies; by far the oldest, I had been told, and the most knowledgeable. I can see him now as I found him a day in early August, sitting outside the cabin sunning himself. He was pulling at an empty pipe for solace; I found out afterwards that he had not had tobacco to fill it since May. He seemed centuries old; his flesh had shrunken from his frame until he was only "hide and bones," as he said. The skin was as brown and wrinkled as a butternut; his eyes were of that pale, opaque blue of extreme age, and they held the same childish look of perpetual inquiry. His lips were shirred loosely around the stem of the pipe, and from under the weatherbeaten hat protruded a vagabond thatch of gray hair. I never saw Michael without his pipe or his hat, indoors or out.

His greeting was the characteristic Gaelic one, "A hundred thousand welcomes to ye. 'Tis a brave day." Then he pulled out his pipe and puffed on at the empty air. "Might ye be the Wee One?" Having settled the fact of my identity, he called in a high, quavering voice, "John—Delia—both o' ye come out, 'n' bring the childher." And then, when he had his breath again, "Here's the Wee One—the Yankey lass we've been expecting this lee long time."

John came, and Delia, grandchildren of Michael's; and the "childher" he had called were his great-grandchildren. At a glance one could read the grim, gaunt poverty that was there. And later, when they took me inside the cabin to see the "wee-est" one in the cradle and have my "sup o' tea," I could feel the gnaw and stab of it. Never before had poverty taken form for me; but here it was hunched in the sooty corner of the hearth, a rattling bag of bones groping for something. But poverty was not the only indweller; there was love. One felt it stronger than poverty, and knew the reason she stayed huddled in her corner instead of stalking the cabin openly.

A brood of half a dozen aerach-shinned, half-clothed children; a sickly, stooping man with a cough and a look of hopeless failure in his eyes; a woman gaunt as poverty herself, flat-breasted, colorless, without shoes and wearing a rag of a dress; and an old man, living beyond his time and need, taking that much share of the food that might have gone into those eternally empty stomachs of the children— all these housed in a two-room cabin bare of everything but the most meager utensils of living. Such were Michael Donnelly and his kindred; and yet I would travel the length and breadth of Ireland to-day if I could only find Michael Donnelly again.

The meal chest was empty, the last pinch of tea had been used; they had boiled their last "prates" that morning for breakfast. This I found out afterwards. But with that hospitality that acknowledges no defeat Delia hung a fresh kettle on the crane over the turf and set the pan warming against the making of griddle bread; while John and the oldest child tramped to the cabin in the hollow to ask the loan of tea and meal that the stranger under their roof might not be sent hungry away. And more than that. So that the lapse of time and their small subterfuge might not be discovered old Michael crossed his hands with the dignity of that traditional King of Ireland and asked would I like best to be hearing an old laoidhe that had to do with the wanderings of Oisin, or a tale of the blessed St. Bridget?

I chose both, and with a chuckle of delight he whispered to Delia, who knelt beside him blowing the turf: "She has the right heart in her—the Wee One. Aye, she has a bit of Irish blood herself, maybe."

So first he chanted the laoidhe of Oisin; and as I listened to those running minor cadences I knew I was hearing the man who had been the greatest storyteller of his time, who had the blood of a famous bardic family in his veins, and whose forebears had sung in the court of the High King. His Gaelic was the purest I had ever heard; and afterwards Delia told me with no small touch of pride that a certain professor from Oxford University had spent five successive summers there in Donegal to learn from him.

"Aye, 'tis the truth," agreed Michael Donnelly. "And,

what's more, he's grown a fair-to-middling scholar himself now."

We had the tale of St. Bridget. The legend has long been immortalized by Fiona Macleod in those rare stories of Iona; but I heard it first from Michael Donnelly's lips that day. Long after he had finished and John had returned with the borrowings from the neighbors and Delia was baking the griddle bread beside me on the hearth I still hold the picture of that Christmas Eve in Bethlehem, when St. Bridget, through a miracle, walked from the Iona hills to Judea while a throstle sang; of how she opened the door for Mary when she came, staying to comfort her, and afterwards cradled the little Jesus on her breast while Mary slept, "tired from the birthing."

I can hear Michael Donnelly's voice now after all these years as he finished the tale: "So 'twas the Blessed Bridget herself, just, that came back as from a dream to Iona again, and her gone a year and a day. 'Twas herself had the telling of the Druids of that first Christmas and the fetching of that word of peace to the people yondther. And to prove the truth of the word she brought, there was the shawl that bound her shoulders turned to threads of gold by the blessed touch of the Christ's own wee hands."

I remember there was gooseberry jam that day to eat with the griddle bread, and I had a new-laid egg from one of the neighbor's two hens. John had been delayed getting home because of a dispute as to whether the white one or the red one had laid it.

There was tea for all, and the family were as merry as if

the meal chest had not been empty, the food on the table borrowed, and not a morsel in sight for the next day.

Luckily I had a crown with me, and when I left I slipped it in the hand of the sleeping baby. On the way down the brae I remembered to make a special prayer to St. Bridget that Delia would discover the coin before the baby woke and swallowed it. When I reached the town, I sent back the "fillings" for Michael's pipe by Mickey, the postboy.

After that I came often; and, having accepted hospitality, I was free now to bring gifts when I came. For the rest of the summer Michael pulled at a full pipe, and I like to think that poverty had left her corner for a while at least and was stalking the moorland outside. Always Michael had a new tale to tell; he gave of his bounty with a largess that made my giving seem niggardly. And when I would exclaim with delight over something particularly rare and fine he would chuckle softly and say, "Aye, ye have that now to put in your head and take home wi' ye." And once he added, "If ye could take the time, just, to write them down, there'd be plenty of Irish lads and lasses across yondther sea homesick to be hearing them."

And next to the stories he liked best to tell of his other grandchild Cassie—sister to Delia—who had gone to America. She had done bravely, married a grand man, had two childher, bonnie ones, and like as not would bring them back for a summer visit before long. I saw Cassie's picture—a glazed cabinet photograph. She looked pretty and sweet in a flat, characterless way as she stood leaning a proud hand on the shoulder of a conscious-looking Irish-man who sat and held a child on each knee.

It was late October when I sailed from Ireland, and the last person I went to see was Michael Donnelly. I think he must have been watching for me, for he was outside the cabin in spite of the raw wind that blew over the hills. A homespun shawl muffled him all but his clay pipe; he huddled hard to the wall in the sheltered side of the cabin, and I had not breasted the hill before he had seen me and was on his feet waving his welcome with both hands.

"Sure wasn't I telling Delia ye'd be back for one more tale afore ye sailed home? 'Twas this very day I said, 'Delia, ye mark me well—'tis the Wee One will be here afore candle time again.' " He was like a child in his gladness—a child who has thrown care and the morrow to the four winds and knows nothing beyond what contentment the day may bring.

It was a day of celebration; we had currants in the griddle bread, and Mickey, the post-boy, dropped in for his "sup o' tea." I was given a free choice of all the stories I would be hearing again, and I chose St. Bridget. With the moor wind caoining around the chimney and the turf blazing high, the children stretched on the clay floor, and Delia with her foot on the cradle keeping the "wee-est one" hushed, Michael took us over the hills again to Bethlehem to the manger wherein Mary had laid her baby. We saw the byre with its rude stalls and the crib where the hay was stacked; we saw the gray donkey munching contentedly and Joseph, fallen asleep; and we saw Bridget stoop and take the baby to her own heart and croon him his first cradle-song. All this we saw by "the light of the Wee Child's own glory" and the gift of Michael Donnelly's tongue.

A few times, from far off, I have glimpsed Bethlehem; but that is the only time I have ever entered there.

It was dark before the leave-takings were over and I was on my way down the brae with Michael's last words in my ears: "Ye'll mind, whatever else ye forget, ye'll mind to find my Cassie. And tell her we're after doin' grand. Tell her ye've seen Delia and the childher, and they were all doin' grand. Tell her ye've seen her grandda and he was looking braver than any one. Tell her that!" And then, when the wind lulled, "God and Mary go with ye!"

When I sailed from Londonderry, Mickey, the post-boy, sailed steerage. He was going to America to try his fortune, and took my address as a chance milestone. I saw him several times on board and again just before landing. His eyes were showing the homesickness plainly by that time, and he clung to me feverishly. "I might be afther comin' soon to see ye. Maybe ye'd be a bit lonesome yerself for an Irish face," he suggested, eagerly.

And I had to agree that it was more than probable.

But Mickey did not come. I made one attempt to find Cassie at the address Michael had given me, and learned that she had moved away more than a year before. The janitor of the apartment referred me to the corner grocer as a likely person who had been better acquainted with Cassie's family than he had been. But I gave up the quest at the janitor's door, went home, and forgot.

·   ·   ·

Christmas Eve came. I was tying up the last of the home packages. I had the usual fagged-out holiday feeling, and the sight of tissue paper, holly ribbon, and Christmas seals made me honestly sick. If I could have yielded up my consciousness then and there and spent the next day in oblivion, I should have been devoutly thankful. There were two gold pieces—one for our old Negro laundress and the other for Ole Jensen, the janitor; and I remember I was trying to think of some appropriate way to give them. They were both in the hollow of my palm when the telephone rang. At such times we always petition the heavens that the call may be a mistake; but it never is. This time our hall-boy reported a person below who would not give his name but insisted that he must see me. A minute or so later Mickey, the post-boy, was standing on the threshold; he could not be persuaded to step inside.

He stood, blue with cold, twirling his cap uncomfortably and dumbly looking at me as if I held the key to his tongue. "Well, Mickey, have you come to wish me Merry Christmas?" I said stupidly for the want of something better to say.

"Not that; I wasn't thinkin' that," he stammered. " 'Twas Cassie. Ye mind—Michael Donnelly's Cassie?" He stopped; his face was working hard against numbness or emotion.

I waited for him to go on, knowing he would take his own time whether I hurried him or not. "Cassie—she's—took wi' trouble."

"What trouble?"

"I'll be tellin' ye what trouble while we're goin' down."

.: 143 :.

He looked at me doubtfully only an instant. "Ye'll go." It was not a question. "She's needin' some one mortal bad, I'm thinkin'."

As I turned to get ready he caught at my arm. "If ye've got a bit o' silver handy now, 'twould come in"—his words trailed off into nothing.

Wrapped better against the night's cold than Mickey was, I followed him into a Battery train and there listened to his story. He had gone to the old address as I had and failed. Then by the merest luck he had gone into the Little Church for early mass that morning and caught a half-glimpse of a face that looked homelike. He had followed it to a tenement near Rector Street and had seen the shawled figure go in without catching another glimpse of the face. For half an hour or so he had hung around the door, and then Cassie had come out. A changed Cassie whom he did not fully recognize until she had gone her way. It was then too late to follow her, so he had gone inside and found the neighbor from across the hall. After that he had gone to his own day's work.

"Her man's dead—died a year gone with consumption. The long illness and the doctor took all the savings. She works in some factory makin' skirts. The neighbor looks afther the childher along of her own for a shillin' a day. 'Tis a fight wi' the wolf from day's end to day's end, and at last the wolf's masther." So Mickey ended it.

What Michael Donnelly had said came back to me: "She's doin' bravely an' married a grand man." And then the message he had sent to her, "Tell her we're afther doin' grand. Tell her ye've seen her grandda, and he be's looking braver than any one." It had been a game of deception played between them with pride and a great love for partners.

We walked a half-dozen blocks from the station. Mickey led the way, always a yard or two ahead, so eager was he to get there. It was a wretched smear of a street; the tenement sagged and smelled even in that clear, frosty air. A foul, dingy flare of gas lighted the hall and did service for the four flights of stairs going up. Mickey stumbled ahead; I followed the sound. I knew we had reached another landing. I was half-way up the last flight when he had reached the door and was knocking; by the time I had come up with him the door was open. I can see the room now, lighted by a single tallow dip; I can see Cassie in her black dress and her red eyes, all courage and hope gone out of them. She must have been crying bitterly. All the prettiness had gone from her face; what sorrow and work had put there had not shown in the photograph.

There was no need to tell of her year of wrestling with death and the losing; or her longer fight with hunger and want and the battle lost there—for it was all in her face for the most casual passer-by to read. She looked towards the open door blankly. To her we were just two figures out in the dark of the hall.

"Is it some one from home—some one from the Old Country?" I heard her ask it more to herself than to us. Then she snatched up the candle and held it where she could see our faces. The flame barely grazed Mickey's nose and his breath made it flare brighter, which brought a little gasp from Cassie.

"Holy God! If it isn't Wullie Baron's Mickey! Lad, lad, where did ye drop from this bitther night?" She put the candle back on the table and steadied herself.

Mickey pulled me into the room after him and all in a breath explained me and the messages I had fetched with me from Michael Donnelly. Cassie's eyes burned into mine; her hands fluttered like white birds over her breast. I could see the cords in her slim throat tighten like whipcords. "He's doin' brave?" she managed to ask.

Mickey cut me short, "Aye, brave as any young buchail! Ye should see him in his Sunday brogues steppin' out spry as a cricket to chapel. And the tales as thick on his tongue as ripe gooseberries! She can tell ye the same," and he wagged a thumb at me. "She was hearing a hundthred or more o' them herself this summer. She can tell ye Michael Donnelly's doin' brave."

Her hands fluttered from her breast to me, and I felt them colder than mine for an instant—"Bless ye for comin', bless ye for comin' *this night!*"

After that she stood dazed and uncertain. My eyes followed hers about the bare room that was everything but a bedroom. A half-drunk cup of black tea stood on a corner of the table that was bare but scrubbed clean; there was no fire in the small stove. Two plain pine chairs, a baby's highchair, a handful of dishes, a kettle, a griddle, and a pot; and across the room a line stretched on which hung two thin little cotton shirts and two small pairs of darned black stockings. At one end of the room was a built-in cupboard. It was on this that Cassie's eyes rested longest. It was so easy to read her thoughts. She was wondering if by wishing hard she could put a loaf of bread and a tin of tea and a bag of sugar on those empty shelves. With a little tired shake of the head she turned from the cupboard and drew out a chair at the table for me.

"Ye'll be sitting down and havin' a sup o' tea," she said it with a smile; and, picking up the kettle from the cold stove, she went out, across the hall to her neighbor's, shutting the door carefully behind her. Irish hospitality held here in a New York tenement even as it had in Donegal; and once again one of Michael Donnelly's grandchildren went out to borrow food from a neighbor that the stranger within her door might be fed.

Mickey broke the silence: " 'Twas as the neighbor-woman said—she said she'd the notion Cassie hadn't a mouthful of anything in the house for the morrow. Ye can see for yourself the stove's as cold as a wet gandther."

I took out the "bit o' silver" I had been admonished to bring and passed it across the table to Mickey. "Being a post-boy in Donegal isn't bad training. They used to say back there that you could buy more for a sovereign and fetch it quicker than another living soul."

Mickey grinned. "Aye, more an' fasther." He took out two bills and some change from his own pocket. "Coupled to yours 'twill make a fair showin'. Did ye mind that corner store as we came through? It had everything from geese to red apples in it. Shall I bide till Cassie gets back or go now?"

For a moment I wavered, and then one of the real inspirations of a lifetime came: "Wait and take Cassie with you. There's a lot of extra fun to be had in spending gift-money." And Mickey grinned harder than ever and added, "Aye, rain has a blessed feelin' afther a long drouth."

It was not long after that when Cassie returned. She brought a steaming kettle and a pot of tea, and went back for a plate of bread and "fixings," meaning sugar and milk for the tea and some jam to spread on the bread. She served us and herself and forced a touch of merriment into her smile. "If I'd known, I might have made a bakin' of griddle bread," she said; and then, "Isn't Delia the rare hand at mixing it with currants?"

Once I caught her stopping as she ate and looking with quick, startled eyes at the closed door of the next room—the room where her children must be sleeping. Again I read her thoughts. She was eating bread that might stay their hunger on the morrow. After that she just drank her tea and slipped her slice of bread into her lap; and when Mickey and I made a pretense of quarreling over the likeliest place in Donegal to find white heather she got up from the table and put it into the cupboard.

After the pot was drained I left Mickey to do the rest. He got up from the table and took Cassie's shawl down from a peg on the door. " 'Tis Christmas Eve," he said by way of explanation, "and the two of us are goin' out to see can we find anything to treat the wran-boys. The Wee One will mind the childher."

The wran-boys are an old Irish institution. Like the English waits, they go from door to door begging hospitality; and bad luck to any soul too stingy to give it. It was Mickey's way of saying Christmas cheer was at hand. Cassie went without a protest, and I listened to their feet stumbling down the dark stairs again. It was rare good fortune that Cassie lived in a neighborhood where immediate necessity was the watchword and where the local trade catered to that eleventh-hour stroke of luck. As long as humanity was abroad the stores kept open. I knew Mickey could get coal and food aplenty; and something extra in the way of playthings and sweets for the children. And thinking of the children, I opened the door to the next room and went in.

They were lying side by side in a small iron crib with an empty cot beside it for Cassie. The room was bitter cold —colder than the kitchen. Cassie had taken the blanket and quilt from her own bed to put over them. I looked at the naked, stripped cot and wondered how she expected to sleep that night. Two piles of nondescript thin little garments were on a chair; two stubbed-out pairs of shoes, one lace, one button, both with soles worn through, stood neatly heel to heel beside the chair. A candle was burning in the room, and I started to get it, so that I might see better the faces of the children; but I stopped halfway. The candle was not just a candle, its purpose was not to give light. It was a flickering little shaft of prayer—a petition burning through a bitter night to reach the all-hearing ears; to touch the all-pitying heart. I stooped to look closer at the small plaster figure in front of which the candle was burning. It was St. Bridget.

Hard as I looked at Cassie's children, I could see no sign of misery on their small round faces. By that miracle of motherhood Cassie had kept them well fed, strong, and happy; she had taken all the bitterness and pinch of suffering to her own heart. The boy was dark, the girl fair; I knew if those shut eyelids should lift I would see deep-blue eyes—Irish eyes; and the cheeks had that soft ravishing pink of a sweetbrier. They were bonnie children, as Michael Donnelly had said—that much at least had been free of deception. Before I went back to the kitchen I picked out a lace shoe and a button one and dropped Molly's gold piece in one and Ole Jensen's in the other. Checks would do well enough for them in the morning. Then I put the shoes very properly beside St. Bridget; the gift was hers.

Cassie, Mickey, and the grocery boy made a gayer entrance than Mickey and I had made. They were laden, so to speak, to the teeth. Mickey carried the basket of food, the grocery boy followed bent double under the sack of coal, and Cassie hugged the precious things under her shawl. Her heart flew into her eyes like a bird uncaged. Here was something more than Christmas cheer.

While Mickey laid a fire in the stove Cassie sat down and spread her things on the table. It was a mystery to me how she had bought them all: two small woolen shirts, mittens, red yarn for hoods, and a length of flannel for petticoats and knickers. "Warm," she said, fingering them coaxingly. And then she passed them to me. "Feel the good warmth in them. Aye, the winther wind can blow now."

I looked anxiously for the toys. There were a drum and a tin engine with cars for the boy, a doll and a small warped china tea-set for the girl. This time Cassie read my thoughts. " 'Tis enough, and more. Wi' the sweets Mickey has there in the baskets they'll be singin' like larks in the morning." Then her hands went back to the warm things again; she caught up the yarn. "There'll be no work to-morrow in the shop, and wi' Sunday coming I can get the hoods done this day week. The last time I had them out the poor wee things cried wi' the frost in their ears." There was no futile wailing over the past, no marshaling of dead ghosts to haunt that Christmastime; only a deep content-ment and courage again to face the days that were coming. That was Cassie.

Far into the night we sat and planned a better future for her and the children—work that would pay better, fresh-air outings, the possibility of getting the place of ma-tron on one of the day recreation boats, so that she could have the children with her through the summer. Under the glow of promise and the warming cheer of the stove months of agony were wiped out of her face even as we watched her. The kettle was filled fresh, and close to mid-night we had to have another drinking of tea. Cassie was turning our cups preparatory to reading a fortune in each when the bells of the Little Church suddenly rang out clear and sweet. Christmas had come.

Softly we stood. Cassie crossed herself, and her face grew exquisitely tender. She tiptoed towards the door of the next room and beckoned us after her. On the threshold she pointed to St. Bridget; the candle was almost burned out.

"Ye mind the story?" she whispered. "Like as not ye had it from grandda when ye were yonder. I was telling it again to the childher last night, and they said—'twas Jamie that said it: 'I'm thinkin' that we'd best light a candle to St.

Bridget this night to see would she find the way here to us as she found it' "—It was never finished, something caught at Cassie's throat and choked the words. She flung a hand across her eyes, and just then the candle flickered out.

I can see her face now as she stood at the top of the stairs and lighted us down. We were almost at the bottom when her voice came after us in farewell: "God and Mary keep ye! If ever ye should be writing home, mind ye tell grandda I be's doing brave."

Hugh Lofting

THE GALLOPING SLEIGH

OTHER KURT, "the Chestnut Woman," was a great favourite with the townspeople for all her ugly looks. In the doorway of a vacant house that faced the Marien Kirche she used to sit, watching the sedan-chairs go by, with a strange, far-away look in her eyes. Spring and summer, fruits were her wares; and these were carried in a basket slung about her neck as she strolled the streets in search of custom. But in winter she was always to be found on her doorstep, crouching over the chestnut-oven with its little fire beneath.

Sometimes the folks wondered what Frau Kurt would do if the vacant house were ever occupied and the nook taken from her. She was a landmark; it is probable the natives would have been as much surprised to miss her from her doorstep as they would have been to find the Rote Turm gone from the Market Place.

Many extravagant conjectures were made as to her age. The oldest inhabitant seemed to recollect her as a venerable woman; no one knew anything about her youth or whence she came, and she would never talk about her past. Certain it was, however, that she was a very old woman and that her language and education seemed strangely out of keeping with her trade.

With the children she was particularly popular, not only on account of what she sold, but also for the tales she used to tell them winter nights when the feeble spark of life in her dull, old eyes seemed for a little to rekindle.

This was Christmas Eve; and though the school had been closed some weeks a small knot of youngsters clustered round the little stove and its aged owner. A hundred yards away, a party of Christmas Waits stood shin-deep in the snow, making an ill-tuned effort at a carol under the window of a wealthy merchant.

"A malediction on their dismal dirge!" Mother Kurt was grumbling. "Did mortal ears ever hearken to such wheezy groans? Music! A dying pig could do better! Well, you lads have asked me for a tale, and I'll not be rid of you, I wager, till I tell one. Yon woeful waits (but not, indeed, their music!) recall something to my memory that happened many years ago. Maybe it will please you—for it's a Christmas tale."

On their toy-sleighs, that served as seats, the boys settled themselves expectantly and prepared to listen with attention, while the fire from the brazier threw giant shadows above them on the walls of the empty house.

"Long before any of you manikins were born, aye, and before most of your fathers saw the light of day, there dwelt in this town a young woman of the merchant class. Her husband was dead; and she had an only son. One evil day, when the snow lay high-piled in the streets and the east wind howled about the roofs, the boy (he was then six years old) fell sick. A physician was called in—an old man who, like the woman, had a cherished youngster of his own. The two lads were about the same age. Over the sick child he worked many nights but the malady grew worse and worse. At last the doctor prevailed upon the mother to allow surgery. This practice was then almost unknown, and men had a wholesome horror of being cut alive. In these days folks think less of it; though for my part, I would sooner die a decent death of the ills God sent me, than let them touch my body with their brutal knives. Well, doubtless this surgeon meant fairly enough but the boy died under the work. Upon that, the young mother, who from the first had been against this butcher-medicine, became for a time crazed with sorrow. And o'er the body of her child she swore that neither meat nor drink should pass her lips ere she took the life of the surgeon's son."

At this point the bulky form of the beadle loomed into the circle of fire-light. He dropt a few groschen into the old woman's palm and took a handful of chestnuts from the oven-top.

" 'Tis high time you shavers were abed," he said with

gruff kindness to the boys. "What do you—on the streets—at such an hour?"

"Dame Kurt is telling us a story, Master Beadle," said the most courageous of the audience. "But 'twill end soon and we will home to sup."

"A fine night indeed for fairy tales," the man replied. "At Hans' Corner the snow has drift a fathom deep. Well, get done with your story, Dame, and let these jackanapes go home. A merry Yuletide to you all!"

The children chorused in acknowledgment as the beadle moved away; and when the huge figure had grown indistinct in the flying snow, Mother Kurt continued.

"Now this surgeon had great hopes of his heir, who in some ways disappointed him. He intended his son for the law, thus purposing to advance him in the world. But the boy cared naught for the dry affairs of a notary; he was all for music. This the father did everything in his power to discourage, even keeping him from school, lest his notes be learned together with his alphabet. But when the parents were away one day, some kind hand smuggled into the house a clavichord. It was stowed in an attic, where, when chance offered, the boy taught himself to play. Through closed doors the sounds of a clavichord will penetrate but a little; and when he was sent to bed the lad would steal into the garret and there strum softly in the dark. Like the blood in his veins was the music in his baby fingers, and harmony, for him, was instinct.

"All this the bereaved mother learned from gossip, and one night—a Christmas Eve—the surgeon with his wife and son made merry in the parlour, toasting their guests. While they were thus cheerfully engaged, the woman stole into the house and mounting to the garret, hid herself behind an old settee.

"When the clock struck nine, the boy, packed off to bed, came creeping up the stairs into the room where the woman lurked. It was inky dark, nothing but the feeble light from the stars through the casement-window. But the lad, familiar with the garret, moved without difficulty among the old furniture with which the room was stored.

"Carefully he dragged aside some empty cases that concealed his instrument, and sat him down before the clavichord. For lack of light the woman was frustrated from her deed; so biding her time behind the settee, she planned to smother him when he went to bed. The chamber that he slept in was but across the landing.

"Then he began to play, softly at first, with reverent expectation in his hymn. So, I ween, must St. Cecilia have played on the keyboard of the Angels. Soon with a rippling burst of speed, he made the little brown keys jump and dance and laugh—in an ecstasy of gladness. Now to a thoughtful tone his music turned, as though he told a tale, with simplicity—for the ears of children. A while this narrative continued in its even, kindly melody, broken only once by a clamour, as of a multitude in praise. But presently into the theme he wove a discord of distress—of doubt, dread, desertion! So it saddened to the very depths of grief, passed, trembling and swaying in lament, through all the dim, grey land of sorrow, and in a deep murmur expired like the distant roll of thunder from an angry sky. Then silence for a space; and the woman found herself praying that he would resume.

"Which anon he did. Again with a tingle of anticipation, but this time so quietly—even as one who dropped his voice lest he disturb a vigil's solemn hush—that the listener had to strain her ears to catch the lilt. Then suddenly he slipped down from his stool, and, standing, smote the keys with his little hands; and from that puny wooden box of strings the royal chords of Triumph rolled, vibrant with all the glory of a Resurrection.

"Thus he ended. With a sigh he gently closed the clavichord, moved over to the window and flung wide the casement. In swept the bitter cold wind, fit to freeze the marrow of his young bones; but he seemed not to heed it.

" 'Christmas Eve!' he murmured, then gazed up at Charle's Wain, hung aslant the sky. 'The Messiah's Birthday! . . . What a story to be put in music! Yes; when I grow up—I'll write it!'

"He looked down at the people passing in the street below.

" 'Ah, wait!' he cried. 'Wait till I have written my "Messiah"! Wait till I have set my mighty oratorio ringing through the world—not for an age, but for all time: wait till I may conduct the thronging orchestra and sway the legion chorus!—Then!—Then you will mark them stop upon the street, pointing to my coach, and cry: "See! There he goes!" (The lad pointed through the window in his eagerness, and his little chest swelled like a pouter-pigeon.) "See, there he goes!"—The man that wrote the "Messiah"—George Handel, the Composer!'

"As he turned back into the room the dim light lit up his chubby, earnest face. So much did it remind the woman of her son, that all her lust for vengeance fell away, and stifling her sobs she slipped softly from the room.

"But the boy heard her. He ran out onto the landing, and leaning over the balustrade, whispered after her into the darkness of the stair-well: 'Who is that?'

"The woman fearful lest answering nothing she be followed, whispered back: ' 'Tis I—Santa Claus.'

"But the lad's unnatural ears heard the tears in her voice.

" 'You are crying! Wherefore do you weep, St. Nicholas—on such a night?'

" 'Because I have no Yuletide gift for thee. My sleigh is empty and my reindeers tired. All my toys I have bestowed upon the other children of the town.'

"At that moment they heard the parlour-door slam below and the noise of someone coming up the stairs.

" 'My parents!' cried the boy. 'My clavichord will be discovered. Stop them, good Santa Claus! My father will be mad with anger if he finds me not undressed. My clavichord will be discovered, smashed and thrown upon the rubbish heap. Nevermore shall I be let to play up here in secret to the stars, to God—and you! Make this thy Christmas gift, St. Nicholas: stop them while I may hide my instrument and doff my clothes—stop them, in heaven's name!'

"And the woman stood there on the stairs to bar the coming of the surgeon and his wife; while the boy turned back into the garret. Of her own danger she thought, 'tis true, but in that moment the lad's sincere appeal seemed to her of most account. That such music as his should be forever silenced appeared too dire for contemplation; and so she waited.

"But the surgeon as he mounted the last flight, on which the woman stood, was looking backward o'er his shoulder, talking to his wife behind. Aloft he held the candle in his hand. He did not perceive the woman till, turning, he found himself within arm's reach of her. But so thickly muffled round the chin was she, the surgeon did not recognise the mother of the boy he had attended. For a moment he gazed into her face; and behold—even while the woman trembled for the consequences of her rashness —*SOME UNSEEN HAND SNUFFED THE CANDLE DEAD!*

"Then arose a mighty uproar; and while the surgeon and his wife descended for the tinder-box, and shouts of 'Thieves! Help! The watch!' rang through the house, the woman crept down and hid herself in a bed-chamber on the floor below.

"Anon up came the parents once again, and with them all their guests. They fell to searching in the garrets, where they found young Master Handel snug abed and sound asleep—or so he did appear.

"With all the household up above the woman took her opportunity; and stealing from the room where she lay hid, sped quietly down the stairs and so into the street.

· · ·

"Now it's time for you boys to go back to your mothers, who are blessing me, I'll warrant, for keeping you abroad so late."

Frau Kurt rose painfully from the doorstep and pulled her shawl about her, preparing to go home.

"But, Dame Kurt," asked one of the boys, "whose was the hand that snuffed the candle?"

"Oh, St. Nicholas, my dear—without a doubt! For mark you, when the woman had regained the thoroughfare she looked back, up at the window of the garret, and from the snow-clad roofs came jingling down to her the merry music of a galloping sleigh."

Beverly Cleary

RAMONA, THE SHEEP SUIT, AND THE THREE WISE PERSONS

RAMONA did not expect trouble to start in Sunday school of all places, but that was where it was touched off one Sunday early in December. Sunday school began as usual. Ramona sat on a little chair between Davy and Howie with the rest of their class in the basement of the gray stone church. Mrs. Russo, the superintendent, clapped her hands for attention.

"Let's have quiet, boys and girls," she said. "It's time to make plans for our Christmas-carol program and Nativity scene."

Bored, Ramona hooked her heels on the rung of her little chair. She knew what her part would be—to put on a white choir robe and walk in singing carols with the rest of the second-grade class, which would follow the kindergarten and first grade. The congregation always murmured and smiled at the kindergarteners in their wobbly line, but nobody paid much attention to second-graders. Ramona knew she would have to wait years to be old enough for a chance at a part in the Nativity scene.

Ramona only half listened until Mrs. Russo asked Beezus's friend Henry Huggins if he would like to be Joseph. Ramona expected him to say no, because he was so busy training for the Olympics in about eight or twelve years. He surprised her by saying, "I guess so."

"And Beatrice Quimby," said Mrs. Russo, "would you like to be Mary?"

This question made Ramona unhook her heels and sit up. Her sister, grouchy old Beezus—Mary? Ramona searched out Beezus, who was looking pink, embarrassed, and pleased at the same time.

"Yes," answered Beezus.

Ramona couldn't get over it. Her sister playing the part of Mary, mother of the baby Jesus, and getting to sit up there on the chancel with that manger they got out every year.

Mrs. Russo had to call on a number of older boys before she found three who were willing to be wise men. Shepherds were easier. Three sixth-grade boys were willing to be shepherds.

While the planning was going on, a little voice inside Ramona was saying, "Me! Me! What about me?" until it could be hushed no longer. Ramona spoke up. "Mrs.

Russo, I could be a sheep. If you have shepherds, you need a sheep."

"Ramona, that's a splendid idea," said Mrs. Russo, getting Ramona's hopes up, "but I'm afraid the church does not have any sheep costumes."

Ramona was not a girl to abandon her hopes if she could help it. "My mother could make me a sheep costume," she said. "She's made me lots of costumes." Maybe "lots" was stretching the truth a bit. Mrs. Quimby had made Ramona a witch costume that had lasted three Halloweens, and when Ramona was in nursery school she had made her a little red devil suit.

Now Mrs. Russo was in a difficult position because she had told Ramona her idea was splendid. "Well . . . yes, Ramona, you may be a sheep if your mother will make you a costume."

Howie had been thinking things over. "Mrs. Russo," he said in that serious way of his, "wouldn't it look silly for three shepherds to herd just one sheep? My grandmother could make me a sheep costume, too."

"And my mother could make me one," said Davy.

Sunday school was suddenly full of volunteer sheep, enough for a large flock. Mrs. Russo clapped her hands for silence. "Quiet, boys and girls! There isn't room on the chancel for so many sheep, but I think we can squeeze in one sheep per shepherd. Ramona, Howie, and Davy, since you asked first, you may be sheep if someone will make you costumes."

Ramona smiled across the room at Beezus. They would be in the Nativity scene together.

·: 165 :·

When Sunday school was over, Beezus found Ramona and asked, "Where's Mother going to find time to make a sheep costume?"

"After work, I guess." This problem was something Ramona had not considered.

Beezus looked doubtful. "I'm glad the church already has my costume," she said. Ramona began to worry.

Mrs. Quimby always washed her hair after church on Sunday morning. Ramona waited until her mother had taken her head out from under the kitchen faucet and was rubbing her hair on a bath towel. "Guess what!" said Ramona. "I get to be a sheep in the Nativity scene this year."

"That's nice," said Mrs. Quimby. "I'm glad they are going to do something a little different this year."

"And I get to be Mary," said Beezus.

"Good!" said Mrs. Quimby, still rubbing.

"I'll need a sheep costume," said Ramona.

"The church has my costume," said Beezus.

Ramona gave her sister a you-shut-up look. Beezus smiled serenely. Ramona hoped she wasn't going to start acting like Mary already.

Mrs. Quimby stopped rubbing to look at Ramona. "And where are you going to get this sheep costume?" she asked.

Ramona felt very small. "I—I thought you could make me a sheep suit."

"When?"

Ramona felt even smaller. "After work?"

Mrs. Quimby sighed. "Ramona, I don't like to disappoint you, but I'm tired when I come home from work. I don't have time to do a lot of sewing. A sheep suit would be a lot of work and mean a lot of little pieces to put together, and I don't even know if I could find a sheep pattern."

Mr. Quimby joined in the conversation. That was the trouble with a father with time on his hands. He always had time for other people's arguments. "Ramona," he said, "you know better than to involve other people in work without asking first."

Ramona wished her father could sew. He had plenty of time. "Maybe Howie's grandmother could make me a costume, too," she suggested.

"We can't ask favors like that," said Mrs. Quimby, "and besides material costs money, and with Christmas coming and all we don't have a nickel to spare."

Ramona knew all this. She simply hadn't thought; she had wanted to be a sheep so much. She gulped and sniffed and tried to wiggle her toes inside her shoes. Her feet were growing and her shoes felt tight. She was glad she had not mentioned this to her mother. She would never get a costume if they had to buy shoes.

Mrs. Quimby draped the towel around her shoulders and reached for her comb.

"I can't be a sheep without a costume." Ramona sniffed again. She would gladly suffer tight shoes if she could have a costume instead.

"It's your own fault," said Mr. Quimby. "You should have thought."

Ramona now wished she had waited until after Christmas to persuade her father to give up smoking. Then maybe he would be nice to his little girl when she needed a sheep costume.

Mrs. Quimby pulled the comb through her tangled hair. "I'll see what I can do," she said. "We have that old white terry-cloth bathrobe with the sleeve seams that pulled out. It's pretty shabby, but if I bleached it, I might be able to do something with it."

Ramona stopped sniffing. Her mother would try to make everything all right, but Ramona was not going to risk telling about her tight shoes in case she couldn't make a costume out of the bathrobe and needed to buy material.

That evening, after Ramona had gone to bed, she heard her mother and father in their bedroom talking in those low, serious voices that so often meant that they were talking about her. She slipped out of bed and knelt on the floor with her ear against the furnace outlet to see if she could catch their words.

Her father's voice, coming through the furnace pipes, sounded hollow and far away. "Why did you give in to her?" he was asking. "She had no business saying you would make her a sheep costume without asking first. She has to learn sometime."

I have learned, thought Ramona indignantly. Her father did not have to talk this way about her behind her back.

"I know," answered Ramona's mother in a voice also sounding hollow and far away. "But she's little, and these things are so important to her. I'll manage somehow."

"We don't want a spoiled brat on our hands," said Ramona's father.

"But it's Christmas," said Mrs. Quimby, "and Christmas is going to be slim enough this year."

Comforted by her mother but angry at her father, Ramona climbed back into bed. Spoiled brat! So that was what her father thought of her.

The days that followed were difficult for Ramona, who was now cross with her cross father. He was *mean*, talking about her behind her back that way.

"Well, what's eating you?" he finally asked Ramona.

"Nothing." Ramona scowled. She could not tell him why she was angry without admitting she had eavesdropped.

And then there was Beezus, who went around smiling and looking serene, perhaps because Mrs. Mester had given her an A on her creative-writing composition and read it aloud to the class, but more likely because she was practicing for her part as Mary. Having a sister who tried to act like the Virgin Mary was not easy for a girl who felt as Ramona did.

And the costume. Mrs. Quimby found time to bleach the old bathrobe in the washing machine, but after that nothing happened. The doctor she worked for was so busy because of all the earaches, sore throats, and flu that came with winter weather that she was late coming home every evening.

On top of that, Ramona had to spend two afternoons watching Howie's grandmother sew on his sheep suit, because arrangements had now been made for Ramona to go to Howie's house if Mr. Quimby could not be home after school. This week he had to collect unemployment insurance and take a civil-service examination for a job in the post office.

Ramona studied Howie's sheep suit, which was made out of fluffy white acrylic. The ears were lined with pink, and Mrs. Kemp was going to put a zipper down the front. The costume was beautiful, soft and furry. Ramona longed to rub her cheek against it, hug it, take it to bed with her.

"And when I finish Howie's costume, I am going to make another for Willa Jean," said Mrs. Kemp. "Willa Jean wants one, too."

This was almost too much for Ramona to bear. Besides, her shoes felt tighter than ever. She looked at Willa Jean, who was clomping around the house on her little tuna-can stilts. Messy little Willa Jean in a beautiful sheep suit she didn't even need. She would only spoil the furry cloth by dribbling apple juice down the front and spilling graham-cracker crumbs all over it. People said Willa Jean behaved just the way Ramona used to, but Ramona could not believe them.

A week before the Christmas program Mrs. Quimby managed to find time to buy a pattern during her lunch hour, but she did not find time to sew for Ramona.

Mr. Quimby, on the other hand, had plenty of time for Ramona. Too much, she was beginning to think. He nagged. Ramona should sit up closer to the table so she wouldn't spill so much. She should stop making rivers in her mashed potatoes. She should wring out her washcloth instead of leaving it sopping in the tub. Look at the circle of rust her tin-can stilts had left on the kitchen floor. Couldn't she be more careful? She should fold her bath towel in half and hang it up straight. How did she expect it to dry when it was all wadded up, for Pete's sake? She found a sign in her room that said, *A Messy Room Is Hazardous to Your Health.* That was too much.

Ramona marched out to the garage where her father was oiling the lawnmower so it would be ready when spring came and said, "A messy room is not hazardous to my health. It's not the same as smoking."

"You could trip and break your arm," her father pointed out.

Ramona had an answer. "I always turn on the light or sort of feel along the floor with my feet."

"You could smother in old school papers, stuffed animals, and hula hoops if the mess gets deep enough," said her father and added, "Miss Radar Feet."

Ramona smiled. "Daddy, you're just being silly again. Nobody ever smothered in a hula hoop."

"You never can tell," said her father. "There is always a first time."

Ramona and her father got along better for a while after that, and then came the terrible afternoon when Ramona came home from school to find her father closing the living-room windows, which had been wide open even though the day was raw and windy. There was a faint smell of cigarette smoke in the room.

"Why there's Henry running down the street," said Mr. Quimby, his back to Ramona. "He may make it to the Olympics, but that old dog of his won't."

"Daddy," said Ramona. Her father turned. Ramona looked him in the eye. "You *cheated!*"

Mr. Quimby closed the last window. "What are you talking about?"

"You smoked and you *promised* you wouldn't!" Ramona felt as if she were the grown-up and he were the child.

Mr. Quimby sat down on the couch and leaned back as if he were very, very tired, which made some of the anger drain out of Ramona. "Ramona," he said, "it isn't easy to break a bad habit. I ran across one cigarette, an old stale cigarette, in my raincoat pocket and thought it might help if I smoked just one. I'm trying. I'm really trying."

Hearing her father speak this way, as if she really was a grown-up, melted the last of Ramona's anger. She turned into a seven-year-old again and climbed on the couch to lean against her father. After a few moments of silence, she whispered, "I love you, Daddy."

He tousled her hair affectionately and said, "I know you do. That's why you want me to stop smoking, and I love you, too."

"Even if I'm a brat sometimes?"

"Even if you're a brat sometimes."

Ramona thought awhile before she sat up and said, "Then why can't we be a happy family?"

For some reason Mr. Quimby smiled. "I have news for you, Ramona," he said. "We *are* a happy family."

"We are?" Ramona was skeptical.

"Yes, we are." Mr. Quimby was positive. "No family is perfect. Get that idea out of your head. And nobody is perfect either. All we can do is work at it. And we do."

Ramona tried to wiggle her toes inside her shoes and

considered what her father had said. Lots of fathers wouldn't draw pictures with their little girls. Her father bought her paper and crayons when he could afford them. Lots of mothers wouldn't step over a picture that spread across the kitchen floor while cooking supper. Ramona knew mothers who would scold and say, "Pick that up. Can't you see I'm trying to get supper?" Lots of big sisters wouldn't let their little sister go along when they interviewed someone for creative writing. They would take more than their fair share of gummybears because they were bigger and . . .

Ramona decided her father was probably right, but she couldn't help feeling they would be a happier family if her mother could find time to sew that sheep costume. There wasn't much time left.

Suddenly, a few days before Christmas when the Quimby family least expected it, the telephone rang for Ramona's father. He had a job! The morning after New Year's Day he was to report for training as a checker in a chain of supermarkets. The pay was good, he would have to work some evenings, and maybe someday he would get to manage a market!

After that telephone call Mr. Quimby stopped reaching for cigarettes that were not there and began to whistle as he ran the vacuum cleaner and folded the clothes from the dryer. The worried frown disappeared from Mrs. Quimby's forehead. Beezus looked even more calm and serene. Ramona, however, made a mistake. She told her mother about her tight shoes. Mrs. Quimby then wasted a

Saturday afternoon shopping for shoes when she could have been sewing on Ramona's costume. As a result, when they drove to church the night of the Christmas-carol program, Ramona was the only unhappy member of the family.

Mr. Quimby sang as he drove:

"There's a little wheel a-turning in my heart.
There's a little wheel a-turning in my heart."

Ramona loved that song because it made her think of Howie, who liked machines. Tonight, however, she was determined not to enjoy her father's singing.

Rain blew against the car, headlights shone on the pavement, the windshield wipers *splip-splopped*. Mrs. Quimby leaned back, tired but relaxed. Beezus smiled her gentle Virgin Mary smile that Ramona had found so annoying for the past three weeks.

Ramona sulked. Someplace above those cold, wet clouds the very same star was shining that had guided the Three Wise Men to Bethlehem. On a night like this they never would have made it.

Mr. Quimby sang on, "Oh, I feel like shouting in my heart. . . ."

Ramona interrupted her father's song. "I don't care what anybody says," she burst out. "If I can't be a good sheep, I am not going to be a sheep at all." She yanked off the white terry-cloth headdress with pink-lined ears that she was wearing and stuffed it into the pocket of her car coat. She started to pull her father's rolled-down socks from her hands because they didn't really look like hooves, but then she decided they kept her hands warm. She squirmed on the lumpy terry-cloth tail sewn to the seat of her pajamas. Ramona could not pretend that faded pajamas printed with an army of pink rabbits, half of them upside down, made her look like a sheep, and Ramona was usually good at pretending.

Mrs. Quimby's voice was tired. "Ramona, your tail and headdress were all I could manage, and I had to stay up late last night to finish those. I simply don't have time for complicated sewing."

Ramona knew that. Her family had been telling her so for the past three weeks.

"A sheep should be woolly," said Ramona. "A sheep should not be printed with pink bunnies."

"You can be a sheep that has been shorn," said Mr. Quimby, who was full of jokes now that he was going to work again. "Or how about a wolf in sheep's clothing?"

"You just want me to be miserable," said Ramona, not appreciating her father's humor and feeling that everyone in her family should be miserable because she was.

"She's worn out," said Mrs. Quimby, as if Ramona could not hear. "It's so hard to wait for Christmas at her age."

Ramona raised her voice. "I am *not* worn out! You know sheep don't wear pajamas."

"That's show biz," said Mr. Quimby.

"Daddy!" Beezus-Mary was shocked. "It's church!"

"And don't forget, Ramona," said Mr. Quimby, "as my grandmother would have said, 'Those pink bunnies will never be noticed from a trotting horse.'"

Ramona disliked her father's grandmother even more. Besides, nobody rode trotting horses in church.

The sight of light shining through the stained-glass window of the big stone church diverted Ramona for a moment. The window looked beautiful, as if it were made of jewels.

Mr. Quimby backed the car into a parking space. "Ho-ho-ho!" he said, as he turned off the ignition. " 'Tis the season to be jolly."

Jolly was the last thing Ramona was going to be. Leaving the car, she stooped down inside her car coat to hide as many rabbits as possible. Black branches clawed at the sky, and the wind was raw.

"Stand up straight," said Ramona's heartless father.

"I'll get wet," said Ramona. "I might catch cold, and then you'd be sorry."

"Run between the drops," said Mr. Quimby.

"They're too close together," answered Ramona.

"Oh, you two," said Mrs. Quimby with a tired little laugh, as she backed out of the car and tried to open her umbrella at the same time.

"I will not be in it," Ramona defied her family once and for all. "They can give the program without me."

Her father's answer was a surprise. "Suit yourself," he said. "You're not going to spoil our evening."

Mrs. Quimby gave the seat of Ramona's pajamas an affectionate pat. "Run along, little lamb, wagging your tail behind you."

Ramona walked stiff-legged so that her tail would not wag.

At the church door the family parted, the girls going downstairs to the Sunday-school room, which was a confusion of chattering children piling coats and raincoats on chairs. Ramona found a corner behind the Christmas tree, where Santa would pass out candy canes after the program. She sat down on the floor with her car coat pulled over her bent knees.

Through the branches Ramona watched carolers putting on their white robes. Girls were tying tinsel around one another's heads while Mrs. Russo searched out boys and tied tinsel around their heads, too. "It's all right for boys to wear tinsel," Mrs. Russo assured them. Some looked as if they were not certain they believed her.

One boy climbed on a chair. "I'm an angel. Watch me fly," he announced and jumped off, flapping the wide sleeves of his choir robe. All the carolers turned into flapping angels.

Nobody noticed Ramona. Everyone was having too much fun. Shepherds found their cloaks, which were made from old cotton bedspreads. Beezus's friend, Henry Huggins, arrived and put on the dark robe he was to wear in the part of Joseph.

The other two sheep appeared. Howie's acrylic sheep suit, with the zipper on the front, was as thick and as fluffy as Ramona knew it would be. Ramona longed to pet Howie; he looked so soft. Davy's flannel suit was fastened with safety pins, and there was something wrong about the ears. If his tail had been longer, he could have passed for a kitten, but he did not seem to mind. Both boys wore brown mittens. Davy, who was a thin little sheep, jumped up and down to make his tail wag, which surprised Ramona. At school he was always so shy. Maybe he felt brave inside his sheep suit. Howie, a chunky sheep, made his tail wag, too. My ears are as good as theirs, Ramona told herself. The floor felt cold through the seat of her thin pajamas.

"Look at the little lambs!" cried an angel. "Aren't they darling?"

"Ba-a, ba-a!" bleated Davy and Howie.

Ramona longed to be there with them, jumping and ba-a-ing and wagging her tail, too. Maybe the faded rabbits didn't show as much as she had thought. She sat hunched and miserable. She had told her father she would *not* be a sheep, and she couldn't back down now. She hoped God was too busy to notice her, and then she changed her mind. Please, God, prayed Ramona, in case He wasn't too busy to listen to a miserable little sheep, I don't really mean to be horrid. It just works out that way. She was frightened, she discovered, for when the program began, she would be left alone in the church basement. The lights might even be turned out, a scary thought, for the big stone church filled Ramona with awe, and she did not want to be left alone in the dark with her awe. Please, God, prayed Ramona, get me out of this mess.

Beezus, in a long blue robe with a white scarf over her head and carrying a baby's blanket and a big flashlight, found her little sister. "Come out, Ramona," she coaxed. "Nobody will notice your costume. You know Mother would have made you a whole sheep suit if she had time. Be a good sport. Please."

Ramona shook her head and blinked to keep tears

from falling. "I told Daddy I wouldn't be in the program, and I won't."

"Well, OK, if that's the way you feel," said Beezus, forgetting to act like Mary. She left her little sister to her misery.

Ramona sniffed and wiped her eyes on her hoof. Why didn't some grown-up come along and *make* her join the other sheep? No grown-up came. No one seemed to remember there were supposed to be three sheep, not even Howie, who played with her almost every day.

Ramona's eye caught the reflection of her face distorted in a green Christmas ornament. She was shocked to see her nose look huge, her mouth and red-rimmed eyes tiny. I can't really look like that, thought Ramona in despair. I'm really a nice person. It's just that nobody understands.

Ramona mopped her eyes on her hoof again, and as she did she noticed three big girls, so tall they were probably in the eighth grade, putting on robes made from better bedspreads than the shepherd's robes. That's funny, she thought. Nothing she had learned in Sunday school told her anything about girls in long robes in the Nativity scene. Could they be Jesus's aunts?

One of the girls began to dab tan cream from a little jar on her face and to smear it around while another girl held up a pocket mirror. The third girl, holding her own mirror, used an eyebrow pencil to give herself heavy brows.

Makeup, thought Ramona with interest, wishing she could wear it. The girls took turns darkening their faces and brows. They looked like different people. Ramona got to her knees and peered over the lower branches of the Christmas tree for a better view.

One of the girls noticed her. "Hi, there," she said. "Why are you hiding back there?"

"Because," was Ramona's all-purpose answer. "Are you Jesus's aunts?" she asked.

The girls found the question funny. "No," answered one. "We're the Three Wise Persons."

Ramona was puzzled. "I thought they were supposed to be wise *men*," she said.

"The boys backed out at the last minute," explained the girl with the blackest eyebrows. "Mrs. Russo said women can be wise too, so tonight we are the Three Wise Persons."

This idea seemed like a good one to Ramona, who wished she were big enough to be a wise person hiding behind makeup so nobody would know who she was.

"Are you supposed to be in the program?" asked one of the girls.

"I was supposed to be a sheep, but I changed my mind," said Ramona, changing it back again. She pulled out her sheep headdress and put it on.

"Isn't she adorable?" said one of the wise persons.

Ramona was surprised. She had never been called adorable before. Bright, lively, yes; adorable, no. She smiled and felt more lovable. Maybe pink-lined ears helped.

"Why don't you want to be a sheep?" asked a wise person.

Ramona had an inspiration. "Because I don't have any makeup."

"Makeup on a *sheep!*" exclaimed a wise person and giggled.

Ramona persisted. "Sheep have black noses," she hinted. "Maybe I could have a black nose."

The girls looked at one another. "Don't tell my mother," said one, "but I have some mascara. We could make her nose black."

"Please!" begged Ramona, getting to her feet and coming out from behind the Christmas tree.

The owner of the mascara fumbled in her shoulder bag, which was hanging on a chair, and brought out a tiny box. "Let's go in the kitchen where there's a sink," she said, and when Ramona followed her, she moistened an elf-sized brush, which she rubbed on the mascara in the box. Then she began to brush it onto Ramona's nose. It tickled, but Ramona held still. "It feels like brushing my teeth only on my nose," she remarked. The wise person stood back to look at her work and then applied another coat of mascara to Ramona's nose. "There," she said at last. "Now you look like a real sheep."

Ramona felt like a real sheep. "Ba-a-a," she bleated, a sheep's way of saying thank you. Ramona felt so much better, she could almost pretend she was woolly. She peeled off her coat and found that the faded pink rabbits really didn't show much in the dim light. She pranced off among the angels, who had been handed little flashlights, which they were supposed to hold like candles. Instead they were shining them into their mouths to show one another how weird they looked with light showing through their cheeks. The other two sheep stopped jumping when they saw her.

"You don't look like Ramona," said Howie.

"B-a-a. I'm not Ramona. I'm a sheep." The boys did not say one word about Ramona's pajamas. They wanted black noses too, and when Ramona told them where she got hers, they ran off to find the wise persons. When they returned, they no longer looked like Howie and Davy in sheep suits. They looked like strangers in sheep suits. So I must really look like somebody else, thought Ramona with increasing happiness. Now she could be in the program, and her parents wouldn't know because they wouldn't recognize her.

"B-a-a!" bleated three prancing, black-nosed sheep. "B-a-a, b-a-a."

Mrs. Russo clapped her hands. "Quiet, everybody!" she ordered. "All right, Mary and Joseph, up by the front stairs. Shepherds and sheep next and then wise persons. Angels line up by the back stairs."

The three sheep pranced over to the shepherds, one of whom said, "Look what we get to herd," and nudged Ramona with his crook.

"You cut that out," said Ramona.

"Quietly, everyone," said Mrs. Russo.

Ramona's heart began to pound as if something exciting were about to happen. Up the stairs she tiptoed and through the arched door. The only light came from candelabra on either side of the chancel and from a streetlight shining through a stained-glass window. Ramona had never seen the church look so beautiful or so mysterious.

Beezus sat down on a low stool in the center of the chancel and arranged the baby's blanket around the flashlight. Henry stood behind her. The sheep got down on their hands and knees in front of the shepherds, and the Three Wise Persons stood off to one side, holding bath-salts jars that looked as if they really could hold frankincense and myrrh. An electric star suspended above the organ began to shine. Beezus turned on the big flashlight inside the baby's blanket and light shone up on her face, making her look like a picture of Mary on a Christmas card. From the rear door a wobbly procession of kindergarten angels, holding their small flashlights like candles, led the way, glimmering, two by two. "Ah . . ." breathed the congregation.

"Hark, the herald angels sing," the advancing angels caroled. They looked nothing like the jumping, flapping mob with flashlights shining through their cheeks that Ramona had watched downstairs. They looked good and serious and . . . holy.

A shivery feeling ran down Ramona's backbone, as if magic were taking place. She looked up at Beezus, smiling tenderly down at the flashlight, and it seemed as if Baby Jesus really could be inside the blanket. Why, thought Ramona with a feeling of shock, Beezus looks nice. Kind and—sort of pretty. Ramona had never thought of her sister as anything but—well, a plain old big sister, who got to do everything first. Ramona was suddenly proud of Beezus. Maybe they did fight a lot when Beezus wasn't going around acting like Mary, but Beezus was never really mean.

As the carolers bore more light into the church, Ramona found her parents in the second row. They were smiling gently, proud of Beezus, too. This gave Ramona an aching feeling inside. They would not know her in her makeup. Maybe they would think she was some other sheep, and she didn't want to be some other sheep. She wanted to be their sheep. She wanted them to be proud of her, too.

Ramona saw her father look away from Beezus and look directly at her. Did he recognize her? Yes, he did. Mr. Quimby winked. Ramona was shocked. Winking in church! How could her father do such a thing? He winked again and this time held up his thumb and forefinger in a circle. Ramona understood. Her father was telling her he was proud of her, too.

"Joy to the newborn King!" sang the angels, as they mounted the steps on either side of the chancel.

Ramona was filled with joy. Christmas was the most beautiful, magic time of the whole year. Her parents loved her, and she loved them, and Beezus, too. At home there was a Christmas tree and under it, presents, fewer than at past Christmases, but presents all the same. Ramona could not contain her feelings. "B-a-a," she bleated joyfully.

She felt the nudge of a shepherd's crook on the seat of her pajamas and heard her shepherd whisper through clenched teeth, "You be quiet!" Ramona did not bleat again. She wiggled her seat to make her tail wag.

ABOUT
THE AUTHORS

BAILEY, CAROLYN SHERWIN 1875–1961

Carolyn Sherwin Bailey was born on October 25, 1875, in Hoosick Falls, New York, and was educated at Columbia University, from which she graduated in 1896.

Miss Bailey was the author and editor of many books for children. She also worked as a teacher in New York and as a principal in Springfield, Massachusetts. In 1936 she married Eben Clayton Hill.

She won the Newbery Award in 1947 for *Miss Hickory*. *The Atlantic Monthly* described *Miss Hickory* as "a skillful blending of fact, fantasy, and woodsy detail—told in prose as clear and delicate as an etching."

CLEARY, BEVERLY 1916–

Beverly Cleary was born in McMinnville, Oregon. She graduated from the University of California at Berkeley and received a degree in librarianship from the University of Washington in Seattle. In 1940 she married Clarence Cleary, and they have two children.

Before turning to writing full time in 1950, Mrs. Cleary was a children's librarian. She is the author of more than thirty books for young people. *Ramona the Brave* was a Newbery Honor Award book in 1978, and *Dear Mr. Henshaw* was awarded the Newbery Medal in 1983.

That book was Mrs. Cleary's response to many requests for a book about children of divorce. Writing in *The New York Times*, Natalie Babbitt said, "Beverly Cleary has written many very good books. . . . This is one of the best. It is a first-rate, poignant story. . . . There is so much in it, all presented so simply, that it's hard to find a way to do it justice."

ESTES, ELEANOR 1906–1988

Eleanor Estes was born on May 6, 1906, in West Haven, Connecticut. She was educated at the Pratt Institute. She married Rice Estes in 1932, and they had one child.

Mrs. Estes had a career as a librarian before turning to writing full time in 1940. She was awarded the Newbery Medal in 1952 for *Ginger Pye*.

FIELD, RACHEL 1894–1942

Rachel Field was born on September 19, 1894, in New York, New York. She was educated at Radcliffe College.

Miss Field was a playwright, novelist, poet, illustrator, and children's author. She won the Newbery Medal in 1930 for *Hitty: Her First Hundred Years.* It was the first time the medal had ever been awarded to a woman.

KONIGSBURG, E. L. 1930–

E. L. Konigsburg was born on February 10, 1930, in New York City. She graduated from Carnegie-Mellon University and did graduate work at the University of Pittsburgh. In 1952 she married David Konigsburg. They have three children.

Mrs. Konigsburg has been a teacher as well as a writer. Her novel, *Jennifer, Hecate, Macbeth, William McKinley, and Me, Elizabeth* was a Newbery Honor Award book in 1967. She won the Newbery Medal in 1968 for *From the Mixed-up Files of Mrs. Basil E. Frankweiler.*

L'ENGLE, MADELEINE 1918–

Madeleine L'Engle was born on November 29, 1918, in New York City. She graduated with honors from Smith

College and did graduate study at Columbia University. Ms. L'Engle married Hugh Franklin in 1946. They have three children.

Ms. L'Engle has been active in the theater in addition to writing books. She won the Newbery Medal in 1963 for *A Wrinkle in Time*; *A Swiftly Tilting Planet* was named a Newbery Honor Book in 1981.

Of *A Wrinkle in Time*, *The Horn Book* wrote, "[The book] makes unusual demands on the imagination, but it consequently gives great rewards." *The New York Times* said, "Madeleine L'Engle mixes classical theology, contemporary family life, and futuristic science fiction to make a completely convincing tale."

LENSKI, LOIS 1893–1974

Lois Lenski was born on October 14, 1893, in Springfield, Ohio. She was educated at Ohio State University and studied at the Art Students League in New York and Westminster School of Art in London. In 1921 she married Arthur Covey, and they had one child.

Lois Lenski was an artist who illustrated all her own works. She won the Newbery Medal in 1946 for *Strawberry Girl*.

LOFTING, HUGH 1886–1947

Hugh Lofting was born on January 14, 1886, in Maidenhead, Berkshire, England. He came to the United States in 1912 and became a naturalized citizen. He was educated at the Massachusetts Institute of Technology and London Polytechnic.

Hugh Lofting was an engineer and illustrator as well as a writer for young people. He won the Newbery Medal in 1923 for *The Voyages of Doctor Dolittle*.

PATERSON, KATHERINE 1932–

Katherine Paterson was born on October 31, 1932, in Qing Jiang, China. She was educated at King College, the Presbyterian School of Christian Education, and did postgraduate work at Kobe School of Japanese Language and Union Theological Seminary. She married John Paterson in 1962. They have four children.

In addition to her career as a writer, Mrs. Paterson has been a teacher and a missionary in Japan. She was awarded the Newbery Medal in 1978 for *Bridge to Terabithia* and in 1980 for *Jacob Have I Loved*. *The Great Gilly Hopkins* was named a Newbery Honor Book in 1979.

The Christian Science Monitor praised *Bridge to Terabithia* saying, "Paterson [has created] a realistic boy-girl relationship, something curiously unsung in literature. [The book] contains a real marriage of minds between children whose imaginative gifts cut them off from others and bind them together."

Of *Jacob Have I Loved*, *The Horn Book* wrote, "The author has developed a story of great dramatic power, for Wheeze is always candid in recounting her emotional experiences and reactions. At the same time, the island characters come to life in skillful, terse dialogue."

SAWYER, RUTH 1880–1970

Ruth Sawyer was born in Boston on August 5, 1880, and graduated from Columbia University in 1904. She married August Durand in 1911, and they had two children.

Ruth Sawyer was a short-story writer, a feature writer for *The New York Sun*, and a professional storyteller. She won the 1937 Newbery Medal for *Roller Skates*. She also won two Caldecott Medals—in 1945 for *The Christmas Anna Angel* and in 1954 for *Journey Cake, Ho!*

WILLARD, NANCY 1936–

Nancy Willard was born on June 26, 1936, in Ann Arbor, Michigan. She graduated from the University of Michigan and received her Ph.D. from Stanford University. She is married to Eric Lindbloom, and they have one child.

Ms. Willard is an author of children's books, a literary

critic, a short-story writer, and a professor of English. She was awarded the Newbery Medal in 1981 for *A Visit to William Blake's Inn: Poems for Innocent and Experienced Travelers*. Of that book, *The New York Times* said, "William Blake, poet and engraver, is transformed into an innkeeper. . . . These new poems, made with adult skill, successfully embody a seven-year-old's imagining of the poet who keeps an inn for the imagination. Color and verve are everything; import is nothing."

YATES, ELIZABETH 1905–

Elizabeth Yates was born on December 6, 1905, in Buffalo, New York. She attended school in Buffalo and Mamaroneck, New York. In 1929 she married William McGreal.

Elizabeth Yates, a writer and lecturer, is a member of the New Hampshire State Library Commission. She is the winner of the 1951 Newbery Medal for *Amos Fortune, Free Man*.

ABOUT
THE EDITORS

MARTIN H. GREENBERG has more than three hundred anthologies to his credit, including several prepared especially for children and young adults. His first trade anthology, *Run to Starlight: Sports Through Science Fiction*, was published by Delacorte Press in 1975. He is Professor of Political Science and Literature at the University of Wisconsin.

Mr. Greenberg lives with his wife and young daughter in Green Bay, Wisconsin.

CHARLES G. WAUGH is a leading authority on science fiction, fantasy, and popular fiction in general. With Martin H. Greenberg and others he has edited more than one hundred fifty anthologies in a variety of genres, including many for children and young adults. He is a Professor of Communications and Psychology at the University of Maine at Augusta.

Charles Waugh lives with his wife and son in Winthrop, Maine.